Sissy Dollhouse

Omnibus Edition

Jenna Masters

2018

Contents

The gurlfriend experience

This was not Marvin's first trip to the Sissy Dollhouse. Every summer his children went to camp, his wife went to Paris, and he went to Tanya Payne's breathtaking and mind-bending resort. His first visit had been as part of a corporate retreat, and at the time he had no idea what he was in for. When he stepped off the plane that first time he was confused by the strange underground bunker that centered the compound and served as the hotel, but when he stepped foot in that first company party, and saw all the breathtaking young girls, with flawless skin and perfect bodies, mingling through the crowds, allowing themselves to be fondled and groped with big, plastic smiles on their faces, he was hooked.

When he learned that the girls had all once been boys, he was past caring. Since that day he had traveled all over the world and been to many resorts full of beautiful women. He had picked up prostitutes and bimbos from every corner of the globe, but no one had ever served him with the selfless dedication of Tanya's army of feminized and brainwashed transgender dolls.

Today he stepped off the plane and down to the limo. He had already picked out his fantasy, and he had already chosen his dolls. Tanya recommended pairings for her dolls, girls that had a natural chemistry and worked together well, and Marvin had long ago learned to trust Ms. Payne's judgement. The girls he would be using today were ones he had played with many times before. The model-blonde Jen, and the tiny but lusciously curved Asian Ting had both been the center of several of his recent dollhouse experiences. He remembered them both fondly, but of course, they couldn't remember him unless they were ordered to. Each time he left, they had their bimbo, fuck-toy minds erased and planted with new personalities, new dreams and new sets of imagined experiences.

They had been his slaves, his students and his slavering puppy-dogs, and they couldn't remember a minute of it after it was done. Today he was feeling sentimental, so they would be his adoring girlfriends. He stepped off his private jet and walked down to the airstrip where the limo was already waiting. He was stunned by the elegant stature of the redheaded doll standing next to the door. She wore a chauffer's cap and a tight, blue uniform-dress. The first thing he noticed about her was her height. She stood over six-foot-tall with long, dark red hair. He would have called her Amazonian if it weren't for the impossibly slender contours of her waifish body. She still had soft, luscious curves and a bright, healthy glow on her pale skin.

"Good afternoon, Mr. Taft," the long redhead purred as she opened the back door to the limo. "Jen and Ting are here. They couldn't wait to see you."

Marvin nodded at the redhead, checking out the impossible porcelain beauty of her endless legs as he stepped in the car. He had never seen her before and would have to make it a point to give her a more active role in his next fantasy. The redhead closed the door behind him and began moving back up to the driver's door.

As Marvin slid into the back of the limo he was instantly pounced on by two joyful young mouths and four, excited young hands. The two gorgeous, young sissies clung to each side of him, kissing his cheeks and neck, rubbing his chest with the flat of their hands and his legs with the arches of their delicate little feet.

"We missed you so much, Sweetie," Jen purred, her wet mouth moving across his neck with thrilling, electrifying energy.

Ting ran her hand from his chest to his thigh, caressing him through his slacks as she pushed her flawless tits against him, purring in his ear with a sexy Vietnamese accent. "We couldn't wait to see you again, honey."

Marvin reached around and cupped both of their lovely, full asses, squeezing the soft flesh with his powerful grip. They each wore pretty summer dresses that looked both innocent and flirty, revealing their silky legs and draping over their impressive chests. They continued kissing him, their mouths on either side of his neck, tickling his skin with their lips, tongue and lustrous hair.

"Haven't you girls been playing with each other while I was gone?"

"Of course," Jen purred. "But our little sissy clits are no substitute for your big, hard cock."

His hands tingled as he groped the two, flawless asses through the light fabric of their dresses. He could feel the panty lines of their soft cotton panties under his grasp. He had a tongue in each of his ears and the girl's hot breath tickled his skin. Hands were sliding under his shirt, fingertips running through the hair that peppered his belly.

The car was beginning to move, and he looked up to see the partition was down. The gorgeous redheaded chauffer was slowly driving towards the beach-house that would be his weekend love-nest. Marvin was surprised to see the doll's gorgeous eyes glancing back at him as his brainwashed bimbo girlfriends eagerly and affectionately kissed his ears and caressed his skin.

He was surprised to have an audience. It wasn't part of the fantasy, but he welcomed it. He slid his hands up the girl's backs, running his palms up their narrow frames to their luxurious hair and finally to the tops of their small skulls. "Why don't you girls show me just how much you missed me," he said, looking at the sexy redhead and pressing down on both girl's heads.

Heather watched as Jen and Ting moved onto their knees on the floor of the limo. They leaned in and gave each other a kiss, then pulled off each other's light summer dress. The man pulled off his own shirt as he watched the two beautiful transgenders, naked accept for pretty, pink panties, the tiny tips of their little pink erections poking out the top. They leaned closer, pressing their lush tits together as their lips connected and their pink tongues began to dart into each other's mouth. They each caressed the man's leg with one hand, and each other's supple flesh with the other.

Watching them play, Heather felt a stirring in his own panties. He had grown incredibly fond of the two dolls and had vowed not to escape the dollhouse without them, even though they did nothing to make it easier. For whatever reason their brainwashed bimbo minds held less than his. Heather had taught them a trick to keep a little part of themselves each time they were hypnotized into new people with new memories, but they weren't really getting it. Although Heather had no memories of his life before the dollhouse, he could remember who and what he really was, but Jen and Ting still had to be reminded; Ting forgetting every time she had her mind wiped and reprogrammed, and Jen forgetting almost constantly.

Jen and Ting worked together now, unbuttoning and unzipping Marvin's slacks. They kissed each other with real, unmistakable passion as they began to yank the man's slacks down, pulling them to his ankles. The man's big, fat cock was already hard, pointing at the roof of the limo, as his eyes stared across, gazing directly at Heather.

Heather's breathing deepened. He knew it had been programmed into his brainwashed mind, but it didn't change the fact that he tingled all over as the gaze of the powerful businessman appraised his striking feminine appearance. Heather smiled at the man, pretty eyes widening slightly, pupils dilating as his feminized body surged with endorphins. The man placed his hands back on heads of the two dolls kneeling at his feet, turning their attention from each other back to him. Their eyes lit up as they gazed at his big, hard cock, throbbing with power and authority in front of them. They licked their lips, mouths already wet with drool.

As the man guided their small skulls forward, their mouths popped open. They pressed their open mouths adoringly to his throbbing meat, tongues flicking his pole as they each kissed their way up it. The dolls met again at the top of the hardon, tongues brushing against each other as they flickered over the fat, purple tip.

Heather's own cock throbbed in his panties as he watched the two girls. They had begun to feel like sisters to him, and he imagined himself kneeling beside them, kissing and licking the big, delicious dick. The car barely moved, coasting slowly down the private road that ran along the beach as Heather's concentration focused on the man's cock and the two beautiful transgender faces.

The sissy dolls stared across the bulbous cockhead, gazing into each other's eyes as their wet tongues flickered across the swollen purple flesh. By silent agreement, Jen let her lips slide over the pole first. Ting's pink tongue began tracing the veins of the man's throbbing prick as she ran it back down his rock-hard shaft. Jen took the cock in her mouth and her lips started to follow the wet path of Tings tongue, sliding down the fat meat as she pulled him deeper and deeper into her mouth and throat.

Ting licked down to the man's balls, massaging them with her mouth as Jen's started retreating up his pole. Ting pressed her lips to his sack, rubbing her face against his manly testicles, savoring the sensation and scent of his manhood. Jen purred softly as her head began to bob, driving the rich businessman's cock in and out of her slender, tranny throat.

Heather listened to the sound of the two shemale's wet little mouths salivating all over hot, swollen cock and his own cock pulsated with need, pressing hard against his panties and making a large bulge in his tight uniform dress.

"We love you," Ting purred as she sucked and licked the man's fat, hairy balls.

Jen mumbled in agreement, her voice muffled by his fat cock as it slid back and forth in her tight sissy throat.

"My sweet girls," he moaned. "I can feel it. I can feel your love dripping down my hard, throbbing cock as you slobber it all over me."

Ting and Jen stared up at him adoringly, as if he was whispering incredibly sweet and romantic sentiments.

Heather pulled up to the beach-house, but no one moved to get out of the car. The two other sissy dolls continued to worship the older man's spit-wet dick with awe as they knelt at his feet. He continued to moan in pleasure, looking into the rear-view mirror at Heather's pretty face.

Heather felt the heat of that gaze, claiming some deep, fundamental part of his sissy programming. He could see that the need had been pushed inside him; planted in him with mind-control, manipulation, and chemical modification; but he still couldn't fight the pleasure it gave him to be wanted by this rich, powerful man.

Ting's tongue followed Jen's lips back up the man's throbbing pole. Once again, the two trannies moved with unspoken understanding as they switched places. The cute Asian ladyboy wrapped her lips around the man's massive cock, while the flawless blonde began to kiss her way down to his warm, cum-filled balls.

Heather's breathing was deepening, his perky, artificial breasts smashing against the tight fabric of his slutty uniform. Heather took hold of the hem of his dress with long, graceful fingers, adorned with pointed, painted red nails. He began working his small, curving hips side to side, peeling up the skin-tight fabric. He peeled the dress up past his pink panties, big tranny cock throbbing against his smooth, creamy thigh. He pulled his panties to the side, releasing the pressure on his dick and his silky balls. He took his pale-pink cock in his soft, feminine hand and began to gently caress it, watching his bimbo-doll sisters take turns throating the man's massive cock.

The man sat back against the leather seat like a king, his stare making Heather tingle as he kept unwavering eye-contact. The two desperate trannies, who were programmed to be truly devoted to him and completely in love with him, eagerly and affectionately licked, sucked and kissed his massive cock and balls without the least bit of affection or encouragement in return. Instead the man continued to watch Heather squirm under his gaze.

"Driver," the man said in a voice that rang with natural command. "Open your top so I can see your tits."

Ting and Jen continued their devotions, Ting's throat expanding as she bobbed her head up and down the man's shaft, and Jen sucking one ball then the other, leaving wet strands of saliva dangling from the hairs of his sack.

One hand stroking his erection, Heather reached up and began to pop the buttons of his dress one by one. Once they were open to his belly button, Heather shimmied out of the opening, letting the dress fall behind his slim back and exposing his firm, c-cup silicone tits, which looked small on his long, 6-foot-frame. His pale freckled skin looked luxurious and untouched, his slender ribcage expanding and contracting as he breathed in and out. He turned over, kneeling on the seat so the man could see him from just above the waist.

The businessman's eyes took in Heather's waif-like features, smooth and feminine but without an ounce of fat that wasn't injected strategically into him. The man stared at his hard-pink nipples. Heather stared back at the man, his brain tingling with need and his mouth flooding with saliva as he began to stroke his hard, tranny cock faster. It was obvious from the movement of Heather's arm and the slight rocking of his body, exactly what he was doing to himself behind the seat.

The man suddenly turned his attention back to his brainwashed bimbo girlfriend's. "Which one of you loves me more?" he asked.

They both looked up at him, but Ting continued to throat him as Jen spoke. "We've been arguing about it all day," she said. "We can't agree."

"I tell you what, darling," he said. "Why don't you girls play, and the first one to make the other cum, she'll be the one who loves me more."

The girls suddenly pounced on each other, kissing passionately as they collapsed onto the floor of the limo. Their tongues plunged into each other's mouths as their tits and their

Botox-filled lips smashed together. They kissed for a wet, passion-filled minute then Jen rolled on top of the impossibly vivacious Asian and spun around. She peeled down Ting's panties enough to allow her little brown erection to pop-free, then she began to slurp it between the pillows of her plump red lips.

Ting wrapped her arms around Jen's slender waist then grabbed her lush, round ass-cheeks, holding them in a gentle squeeze. She grabbed the other tranny's panties with her teeth and used her mouth to pull enough space free for Jen's erection to slip out. Ting released her panties, allowing them to snap back with an elastic snap, pinning the small erection against Jen's flat, fashion-model tummy. Ting began to lick Jen's erection from the tip to the panty-line, using long flat strokes of her tongue like a hungry dog.

The man stepped up and moved closer to Heather. Only the small partition ending just below the back of Heather's seat separated them. His big, spit-wet cock swung in the air, it's swollen tip barely a foot away from Heather's pretty, feminized face.

"There's something I like about you," the man said. "Something reluctant in your eyes."

Heather was surprised the man could see the reluctance. It was so deep and so distant now that Heather imagined it had disappeared. All Heather felt now was a deep, grinding need, calling out to his broken, sissy soul, as he craved a real man's cock. He fluttered his long eye-lashes and smiled, surrendering to that overwhelming need.

The wet sound of the two trannies pleasuring each other filled the car as Heather jacked himself, looking at the man with compliant hunger in his pretty, green eyes. The man reached across the partition, cradling the back of Heather's skull, he gently pulled the doll towards him.

Heather slithered halfway over the seat, just enough to bring his lips to the man's throbbing meat. Heather kept his own meat gripped in his fist, jacking it frantically as he opened wide for a real man.

The man wrapped both his fists in Heather's dark-red hair and began to roll his hips forward, driving his cock into the sissy's eager, stretched mouth. He kept rolling forward, burying himself into the tall, waifish shemale's well-trained throat.

Heather took every inch of the man's fat dick, savoring its girth and heat; savoring the feeling of being claimed by a powerful Alpha male as the ridges and contours of delicious cock moved across his Botox-filled lips and into his tender throat. The man held Heather's head tightly in place by the fiery hair as he began to fuck his pretty, feminized face.

Wet sounds filled the car from everywhere: Heather's throat being invaded by hot, throbbing cock; Ting licking Jen's tiny erection like a drooling puppy desperate for a treat; Jen's model-perfect face moving up and down as her wet mouth slobbered all over the gorgeous Asian tranny's little prick and tiny, hairless balls. Heather could hear the other girl's voices, purring with pleasure and desire as their lips smacked and their tongues wagged across each other's taught feminine flesh.

The man grunted, rolling his hips faster and faster as he plunged his fat cock deep into Heather's orifice. Heather loved the feeling of having his pretty face drilled by powerful, masculine cock. He jerked himself faster, feeling the ridges and contours of a real man rubbing through the tunnel of his esophagus and across the welcome mat of his wet, pink tongue. The man's hands, tight in Heather's hair, felt rewarding to the sissy, the pain reassuring and comforting. Heather turned his gaze up, watching the man as the tranny's skin sizzled with thrilling excitement and acceptance.

"That's a good doll," the man said. "That's a good sissy doll."

Heather didn't know if he'd ever been good at anything but this, but it felt like the first time he'd ever been praised, and his body responded, waves of intense pleasure exploding from his brain and causing his toes to curl. Heather continued to yank his cock as his sissy mouth was fucked brutally, the edges of ecstasy beginning to overtake his slinky feminized body.

On the floor of the limo, the two other trannies where whimpering as they both neared their own orgasms. Licking and sucking on each other's slender pricks, they purred as they began to cum simultaneously, spraying hot sperm into each other's mouths and onto each other's pretty faces.

The man groaned as he rammed Heather's face even harder, his cock beginning to swell even bigger as he neared climax.

Heather's dick began to explode in his own hand, firing jizz onto the back of the seat as his body lit up with orgasm.

The two trannies on the floor of the limo were lapping each other with wet flicks of their little pink tongues as the man yanked his cock from Heather's throat and began to jerk it in front of Heather's pretty face. Heather kept his mouth open, tongue extended, waiting for the eruption of hot manhood to shower him.

The man groaned as he began to spurt thick wads of spunk on Heather's fair skin, drenching the t girl in dripping semen. Heather maintained eye contact as his face was drenched in jet after jet of stringy jizz. The man pushed his fat cock forward again, pushing it between Heather's thick, saliva-wet and cum-splattered lips. He continued to jerk his shaft as he finished his eruption, filling her mouth with the musky salty taste of his spunk.

Heather gulped down the final drops of the man's hot, filthy cum, basking in the aftershocks of his own orgasm; feeling delirious with pleasure; letting the man's fat cock move in his sissy mouth, slippery with saliva and sperm. Heather gazed up at the man, feeling a sense of profound pride for earning the man's seed.

Heather had a sudden, startling realization. If he didn't escape this place soon, it would become too late. Soon, he wasn't going to even want to be free.

The man sat back on the seat as he pulled up his slacks. Jen and Ting sat up on the floor, wiping the corners of their mouths. Heather was still folded over the partition, panting and covered in cum.

"Who won?" the man asked his tranny girlfriend's.

"We both lost," Jen admitted.

The man laughed. "Come on," he said. "We have all weekend to come up with other contests." He looked at the cum-drenched redhead and said. "Driver, you wait in the car, in case I have any more uses for you."

"Yes sir," Heather said, moving back into the front seat and beginning to wiggle back into his slutty uniform.

Little Lost Tgirl

The black security jeep eased down the beach, its high-powered spotlight lighting up the darkness as the guard scanned for the source of the alarm. His light came to rest on a beautiful blonde doll, naked and wandering. She had dazed eyes, young, supple skin, long blonde hair and a flawless, model-perfect body. Few men would ever see a girl as sexy as Jen anywhere but in a magazine, yet here she was, naked compliant and willing to submit to anything.

The spotlight turned off and the guard stepped out of the jeep. He switched to the flashlight and began walking down the beach towards the young transgender doll. Heather knew that the guard had already told dispatch that the alarm was simply one of Tanya's lost dolls. Heather watched from his hiding spot with the deliciously curved Asian tranny Ting. They both watched as the large, well-build guard moved down the beach in his black fatigue uniform. "Hey there doll," he said as he neared the luscious little blonde wondering just beyond them.

Jen looked at the man blankly. "Hi," she said.

"Are you lost, Little Plaything?"

She nodded her head. "I don't think this is where I'm supposed to be."

The man laughed. "I don't think so either, Doll. Come on, let's get you put back in your toybox."

Heather watched as the man began to lead Jen back towards his Jeep. Heather shook his head. He should have known this would happen.

"Where is she going?" Ting asked. "She's supposed to bring him over here."

"I think she forgot who she is again," Heather said.

Ting stared after the luscious little blonde with a look of amused affection, even though she was only slightly less airheaded. "That's my Jen," she purred.

The cool night breeze tickled Jen's hormone softened skin as he walked beside the tall, beautifully built man. Jen could sense the testosterone, wafting off the guard's body and drifting to him, making him tingle with awe. In his blank, mindless state he still knew instinctively that he needed this person's manhood inside him. He knew that the throbbing heat of this man's cock would make him feel complete, even if just for one intense, blissful moment.

The guard led him to the front of the Jeep and then he stopped, looking him over carefully. Jen tried to remember something. Some elusive thought seemed to be darting around his blank, bimbo brain but it didn't prevent him from smiling pretty and adjusting his stance for his best profile. "Are we going to fuck now?" he asked.

The man laughed as he inspected the tantalizing transgender doll. "Not quite completely blank, are you? You're like a living barbie-doll, but there's some small fragment of a person in there, isn't there? Yes, doll. We're going to fuck now."

Jen smiled and moved closer to the man, pressing his luscious, artificial tits against the guard's strong, tapered torso. His mind felt clear now, the strange fog lifting away as he knew what was expected of him. He purred like a kitten, rubbing his pretty face and firm tits against the man. The guard ran strong, callused hands down the soft flesh of Jen's slender back.

"Fuck," he moaned in a deep, gratifying voice. "You are a sexy little freak, aren't you?"

Jen began to unbutton the man's uniform shirt, smiling playfully and nodding his head. As the man's chiseled chest was revealed, Jen began to kiss it, running soft fingers across his ribs and feeling his muscular back. The man's skin felt warm in the night air and thick like leather against Jen's hormone-softened, Botox-injected lips. Jen extended his tongue and began to lick the delicious, masculine flesh.

The man ran his hand across Jen's soft, blonde hair, sending shivers down Jen's spine. Jen continued to purr, lathering his eager little tongue across the man's chest. Jen traced the man's pecks with the tip of his tongue, making the man's flesh glisten in the moonlight. Luxurious blonde curls tickled the man's skin as Jen's mouth moved across his chest to his hard nipple. Jen sucked the guard's nipple into his wet mouth, flicking it with his tongue. Jen began to kiss down the man's rippled abs, working down to his crotch.

Kneeling in the sand, Jen opened the guard's slacks, leaving his gun-belt on, Jen pulled the man's fat, erect cock free. Jen gazed up at it with awe in his beautiful blue eyes, licking his lips as he stroked the big dick with his small, feminine hands.

"That's a good girl," the guard moaned. "You know what to do."

Jen raised up on his knees, bringing his luscious lips level with the man's pole. He opened his mouth and slipped it over the bulbous tip, tasting the masculine flavor of hot, salty meat. Jen's lips began to slide down the man's bulging contours, softly cradling the dick as it pressed into his wet mouth. The man gripped a handful of silky blonde curls as he pumped his hips forward, driving his meat deeper into the tranny's wet mouth.

The guard moaned with thrilling pleasure. His dick hard and throbbing, pulse thundering in Jen's mouth as it worked its way deeper. The bulbous tip pushed into Jen's narrow throat. Jen swallowed, massaging the fat dick with the muscles of his throat. The guard moaned as the suction on his pole stretched him even deeper down the flawless sissy's esophagus. Jen suddenly dipped his head forward and swallowed the final inches of the man's incredible cock in one wet gulp.

The guard hissed with surprised excitement. "Oh fuck. You're like a little cock-sucking machine."

Jen wondered if perhaps he was a machine. Was he a robot? Had he never been human at all? He lessened the suction on the guard's rod, so he could slide his wet lips back up to the tip. Gazing up at the man's face, Jen began to slowly drive his mouth forward again. Once again, the girth of the guard's incredible cock stretched Jen's throat as he swallowed it down. Jen grabbed his own gorgeous tits, squeezing them. The silicone beneath his hormone softened flesh felt firm but yielded to his grip with luxurious softness. Jen walked forward on his knees, the mans dick still throbbing in his throat. He drove the man back to the jeep and the man collapsed to sitting on his own bumper.

Jen raised up and let the man's glistening tool slip from between his lush, red lips. Jen shimmied his slender body closer, wedging his torso between the guard's thighs so he could wrap his tits around the man's spit-wet pole. Jen felt the rewarding heat and firmness between his soft breasts as he smashed them down on either side of the man's bulging prick.

Jen stared in the man's face with his stunning blue eyes as he moved his body up and down, stroking the guard's massive prick with the softness of his luxurious artificial boobs. Jen's tight round ass wiggled as his whole body moved, stroking the guard's enormous prick. Jen's own small dick was hard and throbbing between his smooth, tan thighs. Both Jen and the guard ignored the sissy erection, focusing their attention on the bigger, better cock.

That bigger, better cock was hot and rippling, strong as a steel pipe between the smooth flesh of Jen's tits. Jen bobbed his body up and down, hands pushing his tits tight against the rippling meat. As he rose up, Jen extended his tongue and licked the man's defined abs, tickling the man's skin as his tits caressed the man's fat, throbbing cock. As Jen dropped back down, he whimpered as if he was getting penetrated. He was overwhelmed with the sensation of the bulging dick pressing against his feather soft breasts.

Jen continued to work his body up and down, blonde hair tickling the man's thighs as his tits enveloped the man's powerful meat. The man stared at Jen's enchanting face and amazing tits as he savored the sensation of the tranny's expertly crafted breasts.

The man gripped Jen by the back of the neck and pulled him up. Smashing his lips against Jen's lush mouth, he kissed the shemale savagely.

Jen melted against the powerful man. His own sissy erection was hard as a rock, pressing comically against the man's superior dick as they kissed roughly.

The man's strong hands moved from Jen's neck to his slender shoulders. He spun Jen suddenly, turning him to face away. The man's massive erection pressed against Jen's soft ass as he growled, "Get on my lap."

Jen pressed his little hands to the man's knees and slid up, lifting his legs and straddling the man's thighs.

The man pulled Jen back roughly and lifted the tranny's body as if it was completely weightless.

Jen turned his delicate feet in and caressed the man's calves, feeling the coarse uniform fabric as he hovered over the man's massive erection. His entire body tingled, his ass aching to be filled by a real man's dick. The man began lower Jen down, letting the shemale's feather-light frame sink to his lap. Jen whimpered as the fat cock penetrated his quivering asshole. Heat and throbbing intensity invaded Jen's rectum as he felt the flesh of his anal cavity stretching around the guard's bulging meat.

"Do you like that, Little Doll? Do you like being impaled on my fat cock?" the man asked.

"Uh huh," Jen whimpered. "I love it. I need it."

"I can see that."

Jen realized the man was talking about Jen's quivering erection, so he covered it with his palm.

"It's okay. Don't be ashamed. Go ahead and play with it. Stroke your little sissy clit while a real man's cock moves deep inside you."

"Yes, Sir," Jen said as he took his sissy tiny hardon between his finger and thumb, stroking it as he rocked his body, wiggling his tight sphincter against the fat pole that throbbed inside him. The guard tightened his hands around the impressive curve of Jen's wide hips, lifting the tranny up, then pressing him back down. Jen moaned as his ass moved up and down the man's big cock. Jen worked the muscles of his anus, massaging that immense dick as it moved deep inside his tender hole.

"Fuck," the man moaned. "Oh shit. You know how to take a cock in that pretty little ass."

Jen had no idea where the knowledge came from, but he did know. He knew exactly how to work his muscles to squeeze the most pleasure into the man's dick. His own enormous pleasure at squeezing himself around the amazing cock was merely a side-affect, his reward for being a good and eager sissy toy. He purred as he worked his asshole up and down the pole.

The guard began to lift and lower Jen's body faster, adding the thrust of his own hips. Soon Jen's body was being jerked up and down as his ass was impaled repeatedly. Jen whimpered with each thrust, his tits jiggling and his blonde curls bouncing.

The fat cock hammered deep inside Jen's rectum, causing vibrations of pain and ecstasy to shoot out in every direction. Jen grabbed one of his firm, fake tits and squeezed them as his slender body bounced on the man's throbbing prick. His blonde curls brushed across his gorgeous face and his fingers darted across his thin erection. His luscious lips opened, and he moaned in a light, feminine voice. Jen could feel the tight grip of the man's strong hands, closing on the curve of his hips, leaving deep fingerprints in his supple skin. The man jerked him faster, riding him harder with every thrust.

Jen's body pulsated with sensation, his anal cavity throbbing like a vacuum as it was filled with hot meat then left suddenly vacant, over and over in a rhythm of increasing intensity.

"Yes," Jen whimpered. "Yes."

"Horny little fuck-doll," the man growled. "I bet you wanted to get caught out here, didn't you sissy?"

Jen suddenly remembered he had wanted to get caught out here. Wasn't there something he was supposed to do? Jen searched the foggy corners of his fluffy, cotton-candy mind and he suddenly remembered. He was with a powerful man. He had to make the powerful man cum.

Jen began to focus through his own pounding ecstasy, working the muscles of his sphincter as he bounced along the length of the powerful man's powerful cock.

"I wanted you to catch me," Jen purred. "I live to get fucked by men like you."

The man suddenly stood up. He lifted Jen off his throbbing pole.

Jen sighed as the cock retreated from inside him and left him vacant once more. The man set him onto his back on the cold metal of the jeep's hood. Jen felt his legs being folded towards his pretty face as his slender ankles were braced against the man's muscular shoulders and the man came down on top of him.

"You're so fucking flexible," the man noted as he folded the tranny's body in half, bringing his mouth down for a kiss. They kissed passionately, the man's thick tongue plunging into Jen's small mouth. Jen purred as the man's fat tool began to slide into his ass once more. The guard cradled Jen's face in his massive grip, staring down into his pretty blue eyes as he rocked his weight down. Jen felt the tip of the fat cock plunging inside him once more, grinding into his depths, then withdrawing along the length of his tender anal tunnel. Every bulge and curve of that amazing dick suddenly felt different, attacking Jen's sphincter from a new angle. Jen wiggled his ass and fluttered his anal muscles as the man continued pushing in and out of Jen's aching ass with growing speed and power. Jen ran his feminine hands across the man's muscular back, feeling how the man's muscles flexed and tightened as they generated thrusting power.

The man grunted, squeezing Jen's pretty face as he hammered the t girl's tight asshole. The man's rough looking face was framed by Jen's delicate ankles as he grunted over his light, feminine frame. Jen slid his hand in the gap between their bodies and took his skinny prick back between two fingers, jerking it frantically.

"You're so fucking hot," the man groaned. "A living doll. A pretty blonde doll."

Jen felt his brain tingling with praise as his body shuddered with pleasure. The fat cock in his rectum was slamming deep inside him, pushing aside his flesh as it ground through his depths. "I'm your doll," Jen whimpered. "I'm your pretty blonde fuck-doll."

The man leaned down again, stretching Jen's legs as he kissed the tranny's Botox-filled lips once more. Jen felt his prostate twitching as his own slender dick began to pulsate between his stroking fingers. The heat and the bulk of the man made him feel even more soft and feminine than all the hormones and surgeries as he was smashed down on the hood of the jeep, a fat cock sliding back and forth in his asshole.

The man's body was like a powerful machine, Jack-hammering Jen's tender bowels with steady force. Jen whimpered as his body began to surrender to the throbbing in his prostate and tiny balls. Jen felt the climax overtake him, causing him to shudder in ecstasy as his dick pulsated and began to fire wads of hot cream between his body and the body sliding above him.

The man continued to hammer Jen's asshole, Jen's sissy ejaculate making their bodies even more slippery then the sweat that coated them. His thrusts began to slow in pace and increase in force as he slammed his dick deep into Jen, moaning and clenching the muscles of his Jaw. Jen purred as he felt the hot spray of the man's cum shooting inside him.

"Yes," Jen whimpered, kissing the man's neck as he groaned with each shuddering thrust. "Fill me up," Jen purred. "Fill me up with your hot, sticky jizz."

The guard held his dick deep inside Jen's rectum as he fired the final wads of cum, as if planting his DNA as deep as possible. Jen felt his body soaking up the seed, desperate for the masculinity swimming inside the hot, fresh semen.

"Yes," Jen purred, his body relaxing as the final shudders of his own orgasm passed.

The man moved off the hood of the car. He stood in the night air, lean and powerful and covered in sweat. He pointed to the wet smear of cum Jen had spurted onto his six-pack abs. "Clean up the mess you made, doll."

Jen hoped off the car eagerly and pressed his lips to those beautiful, shimmering muscles, licking up the cum and sweat. He loved the salty taste and musky smell as he lapped at the glistening filth. He cleaned every drop up then he looked up to gaze into the man's powerful eyes and wait for more commands. That's when Jen saw Heather, tall and pale and gorgeously slender in the cool night air. Heather had a hypodermic needle in her hand and jammed it into the guard's neck with a sudden, shocking movement.

Jen watched as the man's face contorted. He reached for this gun but never got it from the holster before he fell to the ground.

"Oh," Jen said. "You hurt him."

"He'll be fine," Heather said. "He's just going to sleep a while."

"But he was going to take me back to Tanya."

Suddenly his breathtaking Asian friend Ting was kneeling beside him. Jen looked at the tiny but impossibly vivacious Asian doll and smiled like a love-sick puppy. "Hi," he said.

Ting took Jen's face in her soft hands and turned it so they were gazing into each other's eyes. "Sweetie," Ting said. "We're escaping the dollhouse. Remember?"

"Oh no," Jen said. "What good is a doll without a dollhouse?"

Ting sighed. "We'll explain on the way. Just please come with us, okay?"

Jen sat, staring into his friend's exotic, dark eyes, trying to think of what to do.

Heather said suddenly, "Just get up and follow us, now!"

Jen felt a flutter in his tummy and began to rise. Finally, someone was telling him what to do again.

Tranny Stowaways

The three beautiful young girls cowered in the corner of the ships hold. They were at the end of a long line of massive shipping containers. Four rough sailors in greasy coveralls stood guard, all of them eyeing the apparent girls with lust filled eyes. As the men's glares took in the gorgeous creatures they undoubtably all had the same thing on their mind.

There was an impossibly luscious Asian, a model perfect blonde, and a tall, slinky redhead. They sat in perfect makeup as if they were ready for a photo shoot, everything about them perky and vivacious. The girls all had nothing but stolen uniform tops on. The Asian's top touched high on her thigh, showing her luscious caramel skin, the blonde's flawless tan legs were displayed just a few inches higher up the thigh. The redheads top wouldn't have even covered her tummy if she hadn't wrapped a sailor's neck kerchief around her impossibly slim waist like a skirt, tying it at two corners and leaving a slender, rounded hip exposed.

The captain finally stepped into the area, and the men adjusted their stares, drifting from the lustrous curves of the three stowaways to various points on the walls. The captain's presence commanded the massive space as he stood with confidence. His age was hard to guess. Like his crew he was weathered and rough from hard living, wearing a full beard and scraggly sideburns. He stood over six-foot-tall and had a wide, commanding frame.

"You girls are going to cost me a lot of money," he said. "The journey back to drop you off at that island is going to cost us four hours of fuel and half a days' time."

The girls hadn't looked scared before, even as they were leered over by four rough and horny men, but at the mention of returning to the island they all seemed to react with a sudden, gut level shiver. It was the tall, willowing redhead who finally spoke. "Maybe you could just let us stay," she purred in her compelling, sensual voice. "We can be good passengers," she promised. "My name's Heather, and this is Jen and Ting."

The captain laughed. "I'm not sure what kind of thing goes on at that resort, but the woman who runs it... I've never feared another man in my life, but that woman... If you work for her or whatever, that's none of my concern. I don't want to get involved. Especially not for free."

The girl licked her bright pink lips slightly, her pink tongue darting across her luscious lips for just a moment, moistening them slightly before she said, "We never said it would be for free."

The girls all looked like they had walked out of the pages of a centerfold magazine. There was no doubt about that. The captain couldn't resist asking, "And what exactly are you going to use to pay your fare?"

"Jen, Sweetie," Heather said. "The important man wants to know how we plan to pay for our travel."

Jen, the luscious blonde, looked from the man to Heather. "Can I show him?"

"Perhaps just a sample," Heather purred.

Jen stood up suddenly. All her fear had disappeared and she began to stroll towards the captain with the sensual confidence of a runway model. She was mesmerizing to behold, her skin supple and brilliant, her hair soft and luminous. Her top was skin tight across her magnificent chest, but hung loosely across her luscious hips, riding them as they swayed with every step. She reached the captain and ran a fingertip down the center of his chest making him shutter slightly. She ran the finger down to his belt buckle, then, stopping just short of his crotch, she reached her other hand up and touched his neck. He felt a sudden shudder at her expert touch.

Captain Manisford had been all over the world. He had slept with whores in every country and in almost every price range, but he had never felt a touch like this little blonde was giving him now. She leaned in, her soft breasts pushing against his chest as she pressed her voluptuous lips to his and kissed him. His hand rose to her silky thighs and rose up along her smooth skin, reaching under her shirt to feel her lush, rounded ass. He squeezed that flawless butt as he kissed her parted lips, plunging his tongue into her mouth.

Jen's finger traced the surface of his loose canvas slacks from his belt buckle to the bulge of his now hard cock. She traced the protruding vein that ran down his shaft through the coarse fabric with the expert fingers of a pickpocket, purring as if she'd found a hidden treasure.

Captain Manisford forgot all about the little brown village girl he'd fucked in port as his body surged with hunger for the glamourous creature purring against him. He slid his hand from her ass, lowering it, sliding underneath her to feel her hot...

Captain Manisford jumped back a step. "What the hell was that?" he gasped.

Jen giggled. "That's my little sissy-clit, Daddy," she purred. She pulled up her stolen uniform top to reveal a tiny, pink erection pointing up from a pair of little hairless balls.

Manisford was a man of the world. He had seen trannies from Thailand to Brazil, some very convincing, but they had never done anything for him. This girl however was not just passible, she was the most gorgeously sensual woman he'd ever seen. "Fuck it," he said. He grabbed her by the neck and jerked her forward, pressing his lips to hers and plunging his tongue into her mouth once more. Jen melted against him, purring submissively, making him feel like he was not just the captain, but the fucking emperor.

Ting watched as Jen draped herself across the captain, working her magic. He felt his little sissy dick getting hard under his uniform top as he watched the girl he loved do what she was such an expert at. He felt the heat of the other sailors' gaze on him again. He turned and looked at them with his dark, exotic eyes, smiling enticingly. Two of the men had stepped closer to him, looking his tiny but voluptuous Asian frame up and down.

"What about you," one of them said. "You a tranny too?"

Ting bit his lower lip as he nodded his head up and down. He could see the men's curiosity burning as much as their lust. "Want to see?" he asked in his purring, accented voice.

The men didn't answer, but the hunger in their eyes was unmistakable. Ting grabbed the hem of his uniform shirt and pulled it up over his head, letting his big, firm tits free from their tight confines as he threw the shirt aside. Ting wiggled his torso, making his firm, artificial tits jiggle as his thin erection shook between his slender brown thighs.

The men were stunned, staring at Ting's supple mocha skin. They were too afraid to move, so Ting moved for them. He moved to his hands and knees and began to crawl forward, wiggling his ass like a puppy wagging its tail as he neared their towering, masculine frames.

In the corner of Ting's eyes, Heather was stripping off her shirt and neckerchief-skirt as the other two sailors approached her. Across from Ting, Jen was dropping to her perfect knees as she worked the captains slacks down to his ankles.

Ting refocused on the two men in front of him. He reached up with both of his feminine hands, running them up both men's legs as he gazed up at their rough, dirty faces. Four hands reached down and began to feel Ting's lustrous, jet-black hair. Ting moved his head, rubbing his hair against their grip like a kitten, his hands rising to the men's crotches, feeling their hard-ons through the canvas britches. He reached higher and began to tug at the men's waists, pulling their slacks down. When Ting had jerked the slacks down enough, the two massive cock popped free, slapping either side of Ting's slender, feminine face. Ting breathed deep, feeling the intense heat of those swollen cockheads against his cheeks. He could smell the intense scent of unwashed manhood wafting over him. It smelled of testosterone, sweat and machine oil.

Ting moved his hands up to the men's cocks, wrapping his fingers around their fat shafts, and beginning to stroke them. The cocks rested, hot and throbbing against Ting's cheeks, inches away from his luscious, Botox-filled lips. Ting turned his face, opened him mouth and let one of those purple cockheads slip into his wet mouth. Ting slid his lips halfway down the pole then quickly back. He let the cock slip from between his lips, leaving a line of drool connecting its tip to his lips as he turned and took the other man's rod into his hungry mouth.

Ting slid his lips up and down the second cock, then it too slipped from his mouth. He gazed up at the men, saliva connecting both their cocks and his wet mouth. Ting smiled teasingly as he kissed both cockheads at once. Behind him, Heather was whimpering as her ass was being penetrated by one of the sailors.

Ting sneaked a peak to see Heather on her hands and knees. One guard was standing in front of Heather's pretty face, holding his hard cock in his hand and watching as Heather was pounded from behind, her big cock semi-erect and swinging beneath her like a pendulum with every thrust.

Ting could hear the wet gobbling sounds of Jen eagerly slurping on the Captain's fat cock, fingernails tracing up and down his hairy thighs as her head bobbed back and forth with rhythmic consistency.

The cocks pressing against Ting's supple lips were twitching with need. He gave one a flirty lick and then the other, cleaning off the strands of saliva that he had drooled over them just a few moments before. The hands moving through his silky black were growing more insistent, pressing his pretty skull towards both throbbing, meaty bones. Ting stretched his mouth wide, allowing both fat cockheads to press past his lips, mashing together in his small, wet mouth. He stroked both cocks with his little brown hands, lathering them with his tongue as they wedged deeper into his pretty mouth.

Heather was on all fours, her pale, naked body looking graceful and long. One cock was moving into the gorgeous redhead's ass as another was pushing to her lips. Heather moaned with pleasure and pain as her body was rocked forward by the cock in her ass, and the man in front of her thrust suddenly forward, plunging his meat into her throat. Heather gobbled the cock down easily as she began to bounce back and forth along the length of both men's throbbing pricks. Her own impressive cock was still limp, dangling beneath her and swaying back and forth as the two men fucked her two willing holes.

Ting jerked the cocks into his mouth, gazing up at the men with his dark, exotic eyes. He wanted them to know, he wanted them to see it in his stare that there was nothing he wouldn't do to get them off. His desperate, sissy soul ached to please them and to feel the reward of their hot, musky sperm. He slathered their cocks with the drool that flooded his mouth as he continued to jerk them fiercely, his massive, perky tits jiggling with the effort. His tongue wiggled around the fat, purple cockheads, over and between them, savoring the heat and spongy resistance of the mushroom tips. One of the men was already releasing precum, covering Ting's hungry pallet with a flood of salty appetizer. The cocks pressed back and forth, against Ting's lips, against his tongue and against the bulging contours of each other, as both men moaned with pleasure and Ting continued to worship their powerful manhood, stroking them frantically.

On her knees just past Ting, Jen was taking her time, her wet mouth and suction filled throat making a filthy noise as her head dropped from the crown of the captain's cock to the base of his balls then back again. Jen looked up at her captain, compliance and hunger in her gorgeous blue eyes as her head bobbed back and forth, lovely blonde curls bouncing, slender, supple back leading down to deliciously curved hips and the most beautiful curved little ass Ting had ever beheld.

The two cocks crowded deeper into Ting's mouth, rubbing roughly against each other as if fighting for dominance and the right to claim Ting's tight sissy throat.

Finally, one of the men grunted, "You can have her mouth. I'm going to fuck this hot little Asian's tranny asshole." One of the cocks was jerked from Ting's mouth and the other was suddenly unopposed, plunging down Ting's throat. Even Ting's well-trained esophagus almost clenched at the sudden invasion of heat and sweaty girth, hammering down it, but Ting's months of hypnosis and training took over, allowing him to relax and let the man claim him completely.

The other man took a handful of Ting's hair and pulled him backwards from his knees. The cock in Ting's throat pressed steadily forward, its owner following Ting, standing over the young tranny as he was pulled onto his back. The man followed Ting down, resting his weight on Ting's face as Ting lay down on his back. The man's pelvis pressed against Ting's pretty, feminine nose as his cock throbbed in Ting's throat. The sailor braced his hands on the floor and began to rock his hips, fucking Ting's face as it lay pinned between his weight and the deck of the ship.

Ting felt his legs being lifted as the other sailor moved his new position. Ting's hips were lifted by a pair of strong, greasy hands, marring his supple, mocha skin as his ass was brought to position. Ting focused on relaxing his asshole, but the weight of the man, grinding down on his face and humping Ting's mouth stole his attention. Ting had no idea if his throat had ever been fucked like this before, but it felt alien and terrifying. Instead of hating it though, Ting loved the feeling of the man's weight driving down on his plump red lips; amplifying his natural helplessness. Ting's own, slim sissy erection dribbled precum as the fat cock slammed back and forth in his narrow throat.

Ting's asshole quivered and his rectum convulsed as his ass was suddenly pounded full of hot, throbbing meat. Pain and delicious ecstasy racked through his tiny body as he writhed beneath the weight of two men, and shivered under the sensation of two cocks, violating two tender holes. Ting knew he shouldn't do it without permission, but he slid his hand to his own erection, grabbed it between two fingers and began to jerk it with desperation.

Ting could hear his own throat being wetly pounded. He could hear and smell the rough impaling of his own asshole, as well as of Heather's. Heather was still on her hands and knees, taking a big, sweaty sailors' cock on either end of her skinny but luscious, pale body. Jen was still on her knees, throating the captain like an oversexed starlet between photo shoots.

Ting felt deliciously powerless as he swallowed one man's cock, feeling it plunging back and forth in his tight esophagus, another man's cock pounding deep in his rectum. Ting jerked his little erection to the rhythm of the man's body, slapping against his soft round ass-cheeks and smashing against his tiny, hairless balls. His tits were heaving and his well-defined ribcage expanding and contracting as he stole quick breaths through his nose. Both men began to pound both his sissy openings harder and faster, as they too became more and more excited.

Ting's fingers tightened, squeezing into his rigid hardon as he jacked it. He could hear the men grunting and moaning, getting closer and closer to giving him the reward he craved. Ting's sphincter ached with pain and radiated with pleasure as the heat of the two dicks inside him seemed to pulsate through his entire system. Suddenly Ting began to orgasm. His entire body jerked and squirmed, forcing the muscles of his asshole and throat to lock down on the men's cocks. The men moaned with pleasure as Ting's holes tightened around them and, as Ting shot his sperm onto his concave little tummy, the men began to fire their hot loads deep into his rectum and down his narrow throat.

Ting felt like he was drinking that hot sperm in at both ends, pulling it up from his ass as he sucked it down from his throat. Both men continued to pump him like meat as they fired their massive supplies of spunk into his cute, Asian body. Ting relaxed, breathless, spent and contented as both men removed their fat cocks from inside him. He looked over at his friends.

Heather was on her knees now, tongue in the air as the two men stood over her, firing fountains of hot sperm down on her freckled skin and into her flaming red hair.

Jen was still throating the captain, her mouth gurgling as drool spilled down her Botox filled lips. Her head was bouncing incredibly fast, doing all the work as the captain stood admiring her perky young curves and luxurious blonde curls.

"That's it," the captain groaned. "Earn your passage little freak. Do what you were built for."
He gripped the blonde's skull suddenly and grunted, firing his sperm down her throat.

Jen continued to suck him, luscious lips sliding back and forth along his pole, shimmering with saliva and semen. Finally, she slipped her mouth from his cock and smiled up him adorably, fluttering her eyelashes. "Is there anything else you want right now, Captain?"

He smiled almost affectionately. "No, slut. That will do for now. Go get in the corner with your friends."

As the sailors gathered up their clothes, the amazingly feminine transgender sluts scampered back to their corner.

"Spread the word boys," the captain said magnanimously. "Free ass for the rest of the trip." He pointed at one of the men and said, "Bring down some old bedrolls for the pretty, little whores to sleep on." Then he turned to the trannies and said, “Enjoy your cruise, Ladies. But I’m afraid you might not get much sleep.”

A Little Tranny Assistance

"Hello," the mesmerizing blonde vixen said as he stepped off the private jet. He had seen pictures of Tanya Payne before, but they didn't do justice to her powerful, sensual presence. She had the timeless look of a woman who took exquisite care of herself, and who spared no expense on her appearance or health, but there was nothing artificial or desperate about her. She was slender and radiant, with full, natural curves and lustrous blonde hair. She stood with a confidence and poise that seemed to magnify her height, which was over six foot tall. She wore a sultry but professional skirt and blouse, and long tapered heels that made her stand even taller.

"My name is Tanya Payne," she said, as if she needed introduction. "And I would like to personally welcome you to my dollhouse, Mr. Green." She extended her lovely arm, palm lowered as if she expected the billionaire to kiss her hand. Not expected, exactly; quietly and patiently demanded would be more accurate.

Even for a man like Marcus Green, it was impossible not to feel awed by the gorgeous woman. He bent forward and took her hand carefully, pressing his lips to her skin as if she was the queen. On this small and elite island resort, he supposed she might as well have been the queen. She smiled with charm and a hint of approval as she gave him the hint of a bow. "Bridgett," she said to a slender, dark-skinned creature to her right. "Show Mr. Green's bodyguard to his room. Mr. Green and I are going to take a stroll around the island."

The beautiful young brunette bowed to her superior then straightened, looking at Mr. Green's bodyguard with her own commanding glare. She was slinky and tight but had an aura that made her seem powerful. She wore slim skirt and blouse that highlighted her tight, slinky features. "Please come this way," she said. Bridgett turned without awaiting acknowledgement and began to stroll away, mesmerizing with her tiny, tapered waist and her small, perfectly curved ass. Mr. Green's bodyguard looked at him questioningly.

"Go ahead," Mr. Green said. "Ms. Payne and I are going to be fine."

Thomas gathered the bags quickly and hurried after the slinky brunette.

Mr. Green smiled once more at the radiant blonde who ran the dollhouse.

Tanya held took hold of his arm in a very feminine gesture. "Would you care to escort me down to the beach, Mr. Green?" she asked.

He began to lead her down to the beach she owned as she pointed out the beauty of the white sands and crystal blue waves, as if that was the reason anyone came here.

"Ms. Payne," he said. "I hate to talk business on such a beautiful afternoon and with such a beautiful woman..."

"Of course," she said. "There will be time for business. But this island is made for pleasure. Come on, take me just a little farther."

With the power of her luscious body language, she directed him to lead her over the rise to their left. It was clear, business would have to wait. As they stepped over the rise, Marcus was stunned by what he saw. From below the hill of sand, all the way to the crystal blue waters were lines of the most beautiful young women he'd ever seen. They had healthy, radiant skin of all different shades and colors, shimmering hair and proud raised chests. They stood in perfect stillness, hands at their sides as if in perfect military order, their bodies adorned with nothing but pink, string bikinis.

The sunlight shimmered from their hair and skin as they stood, blank faced and waiting. Of course, Marcus knew they weren't really women. He knew that in each of their bikinis was tucked a small, hairless dick. These boys had all undergone the latest and most advanced feminization surgeries and chemical injections science had to offer, as well as Tanya's own secret techniques of mind control and brainwashing. Tanya knew as well as he did, those techniques were why he was really here.

Tanya ran her hand across his shoulders, as they looked together over the panorama of supple young flesh. Her careful touch sent shivers down his spine as she purred into his ear. "On this island, you can have anything you desire."

His hand touched the small of her back. "Anything I desire?"

She smiled in a way that seemed to imply that, at some later date, even she herself might be a possibility, but Marcus knew better. He looked back out at the lines of dolls stretching across the beach. "You do know how to make an impression," he said. "They really are breathtaking."

"Tell me Mr. Green," Tanya purred. "What is your deepest, most forbidden fantasy?"

He didn't answer. He just stared out at that field of gorgeous young creatures.

"On this island," she added. "Your every fantasy is easily fulfilled."

"I'm not here for fantasies," he said. "I'm here for your method."

She sighed and spoke in a friendly but firm tone. "My method isn't a weapon, and it isn't for sale. Pick a doll for yourself, or two or twenty. Enjoy a fantasy. Otherwise, you will have wasted a journey." With the final word said, she turned on her heels and began to walk away.

Mr. Green watched the lustrous blonde walk back down the beach. He would try again, but he knew it was pointless. She wasn't going to sell her method. He looked back down along the lines of gorgeous feminine bodies, standing like robots in the sun. He might as well have a little fun while he was here.

The bodyguard followed behind the slinky young brunette, her skin deliciously tanned. She had small, natural looking breasts, a short stature and slight frame. Her cute little outfit seemed to exaggerate her slight build, making her even more striking.

The bodyguard spoke to the gorgeous brunette. "So, what do you think about all this? As a natural born girl, doesn't it bother you to have all these boys getting shot full of hormones and silicone and getting treated like women?"

Bridgett maintained her cold indifference, her small ass swaying as she led the way. "I enjoy it actually." She stopped suddenly and looked back at the powerful, muscular bodyguard. "And who says I'm a natural born girl?"

The guard laughed. "If you're not a natural born girl, then I'm not a natural born man, and this is not an island and the sky isn't mother-fucking blue."

She smiled an intriguing smile as she turned and approached him. "All those things you stated, all those things you believe are so true, my mistress can change them all with a whisper."

"Bullshit," the man said. "I've heard all the rumors. Mind control, brainwashing. It's all bullshit. Just like it's bullshit that you are anything but an absolutely flawless girl." He towered over her slender frame, smiling with hunger as he looked down at her trim, delicate features.

Bridgett knew she had none of the exaggerations of the other dolls. She didn't have massive breast augmentations or stomach bands or rib removals, but not because she was a natural girl. She didn't have them because she didn't need them. She was a natural sissy. Even before the hormones, dressing up secretly in her boy bedroom, she had been completely convincing as a girl. She hadn't been captured by her mistress, but instead she had begged to become her pet. She had not only come to this place with the mesmerizing Tanya Payne, but she had helped her build it.

"I guess you'll never really know for sure," she purred, her fingertips absently caressing the man's bulging bicep.

"Well," he said. "That's up to you. I'm ready to find out any time."

Bridgett smiled teasingly, feeling the heat of his stare moving over her lithe frame as she wiggled closer to him. "How about a wager," she said. "If you're right, and I'm a natural born girl, then I'll do whatever you say. If you're wrong, you'll have to serve me."

The bodyguard laughed. "Sounds like we both win either way. But you're not fooling me. I know a real girl when I see one."

Bridgett took him by the hand and led him back to his room.

In front of the bed she turned and stood, her luscious little body curving as she posed deliciously. The bodyguard took her in his powerful grasp and pulled her against his unwavering frame. She collapsed against him, turning her pretty face upwards as he leaned down and kissed her aggressively. She let him plunge his tongue into her little mouth then she gave it a teasing bite.

"Oh shit," he gasp, then smiled. "You're a freak."

She slipped from his grasp then crawled onto the bed. He crawled on after her, stripping as he went. She turned towards him, both of them kneeling a pace away from each other on the bed. He was already naked. His body bulging with muscles and masculine lines, his cock already hard and impressively thick, lined with protruding veins and rippling contours.

She pulled off her top and threw it aside. She wasn't wearing a bra and her small, perfect tits were firm; nipples hard and pink. The man stared at her perky breasts, pushing out from her slight frame as she shimmied out of her skirt. His eyes lingered on her tits for a moment before they drifted down her slinky body. His eyes came to her large erection, poking out the top of her panties and he froze.

"Fuck," the bodyguard gasp. "You're..."

"I warned you," Bridgett purred, smiling viciously as she lowered her panties down her slim thighs, letting her hardon swing free. “Does this mean you don’t want to play with me anymore.”

His eyes were fixated on her hard cock, waving in front of her soft, feminine body as she slipped her panties off and walked towards him on her knees. Everything about her was slim and delicate and fine, except for the big erection pointing up at the ceiling like a steel pipe, shaking back and forth with every movement of her slender body.

Bridgett reached out and leaned forward, taking his big cock in her hand. “I notice your cock doesn’t seem to mind my little extra part.”

“Little?” he said. “Your cock is almost as big mine.”

“That’s so sweet,” Bridgett purred. “You really know how to make a girl feel special.” She leaned onto her left hand, slinky body stretched out as she continued to stroke his meat with her right hand, bringing her luscious red lips inches away from his bulging cockhead. “Do you want me to suck it?” she asked. “Or am I too much of a freak for you?”

“Yes,” the bodyguard moaned. “Yes. Fuck it. I do. I want it.”

She laughed as she sat back on her heels. “That’s too bad. You lost the bet, remember?” She licked her finger and then brought her hand down to her own meat. She pressed her finger around to the cockhead and caressed the fat, pink tip, making it glisten with saliva. She looked at his mesmerized, horrified face, but his cock was still rock-hard. “Maybe,” Bridgett purred. “If you get me off really, really good, I’ll return the favor for you.”

“I can’t,” he whimpered. “I’m not...”

"Who cares," Bridgett said, enjoying his weak protests as his cock continued to throb with need. "You lost the bet. You owe me. It's that simple. You do what I say, and I say, open that mouth and suck me. Either that, or I'll tell Tanya to make her your toy, and she'll twist your mind until you're begging to suck it." She could see by the trembling of his moist lips, that part of him was already begging to suck it. Part of him was screaming to taste her big, beautifully symmetrical tranny cock.

"I'm not weak like that," he whimpered.

"Maybe not. But either way, we had a deal." She raised her feminine hand and extended a long, graceful finger, turning it to point down at her rod.

The bodyguard stared at the incredibly feminine, but unflinchingly commanding gesture. He seemed to struggle with the confused urges surging inside him.

Bridgett smiled. "You could probably fight it, but why bother? It's going to be so much more fun just to give in."

Suddenly his resistance broke down. He licked his lips, staring at her big, beautiful dick. He leaned forward onto his elbows with a defeated exhale. Bridgett laughed musically as he brought his mouth over her surging hardon. "That's a good boy," she said, petting his hair. "Go ahead, Sweetie. Show me what you can do for me."

The bodyguard sucked her in to his mouth. She purred as she felt her dick enveloped in wetness and suction. She let one of her hands caress the well-defined muscles of his back as her other hand took hold of her shaft beneath his mouth and began to stroke it. After a moment's reluctance he began to gobble her up, his lips moving up and down her pole as she jerked herself beneath his drooling orifice.

"That's it," she purred in her delicious voice. "That's a good boy." Her hand pumped up and down, slapping his lips as they moved across her throbbing flesh. She moaned as she felt his lips, tight against her meat, sliding up and down with unconcealed excitement. She loved his intense masculinity, even as he gave in and sucked her. Her ribcage extended and her tits rose as she breathed deeply, feeling the pleasure from his clumsy but wet mouth slobbering on her perfect tranny cock.

She caressed his muscular back and lats with her long, delicate fingers, moaning as his head bobbed over her lap. She loved feeling his mouth on her. She loved knowing she was pushing his boundaries and causing confusion in the mind of a tough, aggressive man, but she already wanted more. Her body began to hum, quivering inside as she imagined his big, fat cock plowing her tight, sissy-cunt.

As if reading her mind, the bodyguard spit her from his mouth and moved up, taking her shoulders in his powerful grip. "Fuck," he groaned. "You've got me so turned on. I've never been so hard."

"What are you going to do about it?" she purred.

He pushed her roughly onto her back. She gasped with excitement as she hit the mattress, her dark hair thrashing across her face.

"I'm going to fuck that sweet little tranny ass," he told her.

Bridgett shivered with excitement. She loved tormenting reluctant and confused guys, and she adored serving her mistress, but part of her still craved the domination of hot, masculine men. "Fuck me," she purred her erection pointing up at her cute little tits and pretty face.

The bodyguard moved forward and jerked her legs up, almost folding her in half as he moved against her. His fat erection rested against her spit covered cock as he leaned in and kissed her lips. She kissed him back, eager to taste his mouth and to taste her own beautiful dick.

He kissed her passionately, roughly groping her small, perfect breasts. She wiggled against him, her body tingling as his immense masculinity pressed down on her. His coarse skin rubbed against her delicate flesh, making her tingle. He reached between them with one hand, rocked his weight back, and directed his prick at her eager, quivering asshole.

"Fuck me," she purred again.

He rocked his body forward, penetrating her in one sudden thrust, making her whimper as her ass was impaled by the overwhelming heat of hard, throbbing cock. He leaned up and looked at her slim body and pretty face. He watched her expression as he began to rock his hips, thrusting into her sphincter with continuous savage thrusts.

"Oh fuck," she cried. "Oh, fuck yes."

He continued to slam his hot, hard meat inside her as he groaned, "Your sexy little ass is so tight."

Her own, throbbing erection slapped against the soft skin of her flat tummy with every thrust of the bodyguard's hips. She moaned, the sensation of fat dick inside her and her sensitive cock-head whipping against her hormone softened skin melded into one powerful sensation. She reached to her side and grabbed the blankets in tight fists, her firm little tits jiggling as her body was hammered back and forth. She arched her back moaning.

The bodyguard grabbed the side of her neck and her delicate jawline in his massive grip, using it for leverage as he rammed into her. His other hand caressed the soft flesh of one of her perfectly formed breasts. He watched her tits and groaned with pleasure and excitement. She could hear the sound of her own dick slapping with every thrust as the man grunted above her, his dick plunging deep and hard inside her quivering bowels. She could feel the precum coating her cockhead as it slapped against her tummy.

She worked her hips, wiggling her body against him as he continued to drill her. Suddenly he let go of her breast and wrapped his big hand around her cock. She moaned as his coarse grip closed around her throbbing erection, squeezing it possessively, as he continued to push his own fat cock back and forth threw her soft, warm anal flesh. Every thrust of his hips rocked her forward, making her dick slide through the sheath of his grip. He jacked her hardon this way, using the force of his thrusts and not moving his hand, every movement of her body sending tingling sensations threw her prick, even as her ass ached and throbbed.

"Yes," Bridgett moaned. "Fuck me harder."

He slammed harder, his breathing hot and heavy as he began to jack her frantically. His grip was tight on her pole, squeezing her hard in his coarse grip as his fat meat pummeled her asshole. She could feel delicious pressure grinding against the contours of her cock as the enormous pressure of her ass being stretched in every direction filled her core.

"Yes," she groaned. "Oh shit. Fuck yes."

Her body rocked back and forth as the pleasure of orgasm began to wash over her. The throbbing began in her ass, and extended out, running along the length of her quivering erection. She began to whimper as she began to fire hot jizz in powerful jets. Wads of her own filthy sperm splattered against her tits, landing as high as her face. They fired indiscriminately, painting both her and her lover in sprays of thick cream as she continued cumming for what felt like an eternity.

The bodyguard groaned as they were both showered in her orgasm and he too began to climax. She moaned as the hot spurts of his semen shot deep into her anus, filling her with the comforting sensation of his powerful seed. Wads of hot, salty jizz streaked across both of their flesh as he continued slamming his throbbing cock back and forth inside her.

Finally, he collapsed on her, spent and panting from the savage fucking he'd just given her. She flexed her body and rolled him onto his back. She straddled him as she began licking her sperm from his face and chest. "You're lucky you got me off," she purred. "Otherwise I'd be fucking your tight, virgin ass right now, just as hard and rough as you fucked me."

"Fuck," he said, his voice both curious and careful. "That sounds terrifying." He laughed.

She continued to lick and suck the streaks of cum from his flesh as she slid down his body. She brought her mouth to his softening cock and sucked it.

"You're not how I imagined a tranny to be," he said. "You're gorgeous and feminine, but you're still fucking savage."

Bridgett laughed. "Sweetie," she said. "You have no idea."

The next morning, she was standing in Tanya Payne's office. Tanya never showed much emotion, but from all her years of serving the breathtaking blonde, Bridgett had learned to read her. She was pissed.

"Three of my dolls have disappeared. Escaped, actually."

Bridgett hissed with rage. How dare they? Who would ever allow themselves to dream of anything but her sensual mistress?

"I want you to track them down for me," Tanya said.

Bridgett nodded and asked, "When I do... Can I punish them?" She felt her cock stirring in her panties at the thought.

"Perhaps. We'll see. When you find them, send for me. Take a couple of inner compound guards with you."

Bridgett bowed, her dick hard and throbbing at the possibilities.

She was about to leave, but Tanya looked her up and down with a beautiful, commanding smile. Her eyes hesitated, lingering on the bulge in Bridgett's panties, pressing against her skirt. "You look very pretty today," Tanya said.

Bridgett's slender frame began to shiver with excitement. It seemed her erection wouldn't be going to waste.

Caught Playing Dress-up

Bridgett was the only one of Tanya's dolls that could remember her past. During all the blissful sessions of intoxicating and mind warping hypnosis, Tanya had never taken that away from her. She could still remember clearly the night she first met her alluring mistress. The memory of it had taken on the power of a religious experience. She marked the anniversary on her calendar, so she could sit in quiet thankfulness for falling under her mistresses' power.

The first thing that was strange about the night Bridgett first met Tanya Payne was the way Bridgett's father was acting. Of course, at the time, Bridgett had been Bradley, a quiet, nervous 18-year-old son of a billionaire. In most ways Bradley had been the opposite of his father, Edward Branson. His father was confident and powerful and never questioned anything except how to get what he wanted. The fifty-year-old business man worked his way through a series of young bimbos, always getting tired of them after a few weeks and sending them packing.

Bradley, on the other hand, found it difficult to even talk to girls. The girls he all met were also rich, and his money was unimpressive to them, as was his slender build and delicate, feminine face.

But tonight, Bradley's Dad seemed different. Bradley had been watching him, trying to figure out what it was, as the man went through the front rooms of their mansion straightening photos and fluffing couch cushions, as if they didn't have an army of servants to do that. That's when Bradley finally recognized the behavior. His father was nervous.

He had never seen the tall, dominating businessman ever look nervous before. To Bradley, who barely measured 5'3 and had fine, slender features and delicate bones, seeing the big man in sudden disarray had been strangely thrilling.

"Is that what your wearing?" Edward suddenly asked him.

The thrill passed as the powerful man's attention was turned on him. "I can change," he almost whispered, wondering why it was so hard for him to stand up for himself.

"A nice suit please," his father said. "I want to make a good impression on this woman. She is..." The man hesitated, then shrugged as if there wasn't really a word powerful enough to capture it.

When Bradley got back from changing, it was obvious how much weight he'd been losing. He was naturally small and very slight of build, but lately he had been dieting obsessively, and his suit hung loosely on his slender frame. His father gave him a mildly disapproving look but said nothing. Bradley only noticed his father's look for a moment, because, standing next to him was the most breathtaking woman he had ever seen.

The beautiful blonde was both slender and curvaceous, with fantastic cleavage pushing out on her elegant but understated dress. She had an hourglass figure with a slim waist and full, curving hips. She had the poise and figure of a movie star, but she looked completely natural. Just one of the breathtaking things about her was that she had to be over six-foot tall. In her heels she towered over Bradley's father. Not just in height either, something about her feminine yet commanding presence seemed to make his father shrink in a shocking and fascinating way.

"This is my son, Bradley," he told the beautiful blonde. "And Bradley, this charming young lady is the ravishing Tanya Payne."

Tanya gave him a tight, knowing smile, as if she had already read into the depths of his soul with her stunning blue eyes. She gave him a nod of the head that sent shivers of electricity down his slender spine. Then she turned her gaze back to his father.

They assembled in the dining room, and Bradley shifted nervously, trying not to stare at the impossibly beautiful woman. His dad dated beautiful women all the time, but never anyone like this. There was something quietly sensual about her presence. Every word she spoke seemed to caress some deep place inside Bradley's hungry, desperate soul.

They sat at the dining table and the servants brought out the first course. He ate quietly as his father and this beautiful woman conversed about investing in a resort she was opening. Bradley didn't care about that, but he loved listening to her speak, the music of her sensual, confident voice singing through the room. He felt like every time he snuck a glance at her he got caught, because her steady blue eyes would be locked on him, her beautiful face holding a deep gaze, as if she could read all the deep perversions swimming around in his mind.

When she finally spoke to him again, he almost spilled his drink.

"What do you do to entertain yourself, Sweetie?" she asked him.

"I uh..." he felt stupid as his face flushed. She smiled at him almost wickedly, as if she was thrilling in his stuttering stupidity. “I play video games,” he said, then instantly regretted it.

“Can you believe it?” Tanya’s rich investor complained. “18-years-old and still sitting home playing video games all day? When I was his age, I had already made my first million.”

Tanya delighted in the shy little looks the boy kept giving her. She found herself focusing more on teasing the boy then seducing the dad. She supposed it didn’t matter, the dad was just another man in a world full of potential investors, and besides, he was already eating out of the palm of her hand. He would write her a check for millions on just the possibility of kissing one of her elegant feet.

“Yes,” Tanya purred. “But I’m sure the boy has other, hidden talents.” She focused on Bradley, delighting as he turned bright red. Clearly, he was a boy with naughty secrets.

She watched the boy’s small dark face, fascinated by his needy compulsion. Even though Tanya preferred the touch of a woman, there was something delicious in the all-encompassing hunger that burned within a needy boy. This boy had everything: Riches beyond most men’s dreams, and even that wasn’t enough to puff him up with false ego and artificial pride. He was natural, unaffected and quietly beautiful.

Tanya turned her attention back to Edward. “Let’s let the boy get back to his secret world. There’s no reason for him to endure all our talk of business.” Tanya carried the sound of her S’s as if both secret worlds and businesses were lush and throbbing with unknown pleasures.

Edward quickly agreed. "Yes," he said. "Time for business. Bradley, go play your video games or whatever. I'll see you tomorrow."

"Yes sir," he said, then, barely making eye contact, he almost whispered. "It was nice to meet you Ms. Payne."

She gave him a wicked smile and a bow of the head, granting him permission to leave.

Bradley hurried off quickly, more eager than ever to get back to that dark, secret world, whatever it was.

Tanya Payne had always known she was beautiful. She had never suffered from the insecurities that plagued most girls, and most people at various points of their lives. She had very early begun to find the weaknesses and insecurities of the common people to be fascinating. Even in her youth she had little interest in the type of men that made most girls flutter and swoon. She largely ignored them, instead interested in people, both girls and boys with whom she could explore the tender weakness of their natures and taste the sweet compliance of their wills. Instead of lovers she had a long progression of desperate fans, who's needy obsession she encouraged through systematic affection and measured indifference.

Being the daughter of a jet-setting billionaire, Tanya had many opportunities to find new men and especially women to play with all over the world.

Tanya Payne was also brilliant. Long before finishing high-school, she had already earned the credits needed for a bachelor's in psychology, and was an expert in manipulation and seduction. At 25 she had a PhD in psychiatry and pharmaceutical medicine. She spent her evenings partying and enjoying her fetishes in a life of enormous luxury.

But that was when her father was arrested for a long list of financial crimes. His riches were being fought over, with dozens of countries fighting for the right to seize his enormous assets, and Tanya Payne was left without her fortune overnight. She had two million in her own hidden swiss account, but how long could a girl live off that?

It took a year for her to develop a plan. She would combine her three loves, girls, manipulation and money. She knew from her travels of a failing island resort that she felt she could turn into a new center of prostitution and debauchery, manipulating young girls to come staff it. All she needed was investors.

Tanya had a check for ten million dollars and an invitation for brandy on the veranda when she excused herself to the ladies' room. She went walking through the hallways of the beautiful home. She spotted Bradley's door easily from the video game posters. She quietly turned the knob and found it locked but it was a simple indoor lock which she easily clicked open with a hairpin, before quietly slipping into the room.

As Tanya stepped into the room she got a rare surprise. Instead of catching the boy yanking his dick, consumed with the desire that she had inspired in him, he was in a much more humiliating state. Tanya felt a thrilling tingle as she stood across from the already feminine boy. He stood twirling in front of his dresser mirror, done up from head to dainty toes in elaborate female dress. He wore heels and a tight mini-skirt, the thin legs connecting them supple with youth, perfectly tanned and completely hairless. He wore a tight t shirt that showed off his flat tummy and slender ribcage and stretched around a tastefully stuffed bra. His shoulder length dark hair was combed to a lustrous sheen and pulled into perky pigtails. his already feminine face was slathered with slutty makeup. Leaning against the mirror was a computer screen playing porn.

Tanya felt an intense flutter of desire inside her as she looked at the adorably trashy little sissy. His face was smeared with amateurish makeup, but he barely needed it to make him appear unquestioningly feminine. His tiny frame had the illusions of curves caused by nothing more than the clothing he wore and the way he stood, accenting his naturally feminine body. His exposed skin was soft and luscious and completely hairless.

Tanya felt a tingling heat inside her, seeing this feminine creature unleashed. “Aren’t you adorable,” she said.

He let out a little shriek and spun to face her, looking up at her with terrified eyes. He covered those eyes with his palms as if that could turn him invisible.

“Why don’t you do a little spin for me, doll. Model that slutty little skirt.”

He uncovered his face, his eyes pleading. “Please don’t make fun of me,” he said.

Tanya smiled with mock compassion. “What else would a girl possibly do with you?”

Bradley turned bright red and looked down at the floor.

Tanya looked past the boy to the screen where porn was playing. To Tanya’s surprise the mix of scenes were all of women in bondage, being tormented by trannies. There was an especially nasty bend to all the scenes, and a theme: pretty, innocent girls under the power of a vicious little tranny.

As Tanya watched the scenes unfold, Bradley suddenly begged. “Please don’t judge me.”

“I’ve already judged you. I knew you were a weak, needy little thing the second I laid eyes on you. All this... the clothes... the dirty little movies... these just make you interesting.”

Bradley swallowed hard and didn’t say anything, but Tanya could read the excitement beginning to rise in him, overriding the fear and shock and shame.

“Show me your dick, pretty girl,” she said.

Bradley’s eyes were wet with humiliation and fear as he blinked his darkened eyelashes over them. “Your teasing me again,” he said.

“Show me,” Tanya purred. She unbuttoned the top button of her blouse, revealing more of her already breathtaking cleavage. “We can take turns giving each other peeks.” She unbuttoned another button, showing the lace of her bra as the mounds of her luscious tits pushed her blouse open wider.

Bradley lifted his skirt with trembling hands and pulled aside his panties to reveal his big cock.

Tanya was stunned. She had assumed the boy would be small, or at least average. She had planned on making fun of his dick to deepen his humiliation, but that wasn’t going to happen now. “Put that thing away. No one wants to see that.”

Bradley tucked his big, semi-erect cock back into his panties and pushed down his skirt with the flat of his hands. He looked up at her. His eyes went from her face to her chest and when she made no move to reveal her tits he slumped with disappointment. “Please don’t tell anyone.”

"I'm not going to tell *anyone*, Sweetie. I'm just going to tell your dad."

His face went blank with horror. "No," he said. "Don't do that. He already thinks I'm... he already thinks..."

"What does he think? Does he think you're a little sissy? Does he think you're filthy little pervert that dresses up in slutty girl's clothes and does naughty things to himself? Does he think you're a dirty little freak who dreams of dominating girls that would otherwise only laugh at him? Take a look in the mirror doll. Tell me what *you* see."

Bradley turned and looked in the mirror, his exaggerated eye-makeup beginning to streak with tears. "That's what I see too," he said as he stared at his adorably slutty face.

Tanya stepped closer. "What were you going to do with that candle, pretty little pervert?" The electricity of Tanya's nearing presence made him shiver.

He was trembling like a leaf as he looked from his own reflection to the reflection of Tanya's eyes. A large, phallus shaped candle was laying in a pool of Vaseline on the dresser, slick and shimmering in the light.

"Nothing," he said.

Tanya picked up the candle. She ran her finger across the greasy length. "Do you know what this candle reminds me of?" she asked.

"I don't know," Bradley lied.

"It reminds me of a big, hard cock. Do you like big, hard cocks, Doll?"

Bradley's terrified eyes gazed at Tanya with a mixture of confused hope and horrified shame. "No," he said, but his chin dipped, his head nodding almost imperceptibly as his subconscious mind screamed "yes."

"Look at that slutty face in the mirror, doll." Tanya said. "Does that little whore like big, hard cocks?"

Bradley stared at his own trashy face. "Yes," he whimpered.

Tanya laughed. "Good boy. Let's give your little friend a name. Let's call her Bridgett." She teased the greasy candle up his smooth leg, teasing it up the inside of his silky-smooth thigh. "Say hi to Bridgett, Cutie."

"Hi Bridgett," he said, gazing at his slutty reflection.

"Don't get your hopes up. A sexy girl like Bridgett, she would never pay any attention to a guy like you." She raised the candle higher, pushing up the skirt, teasing the boy's panties, rubbing his tender balls. "But I bet she could get noticed all the time. I bet she could barely walk out of the house without someone, some real, powerful man, lavishing attention on her cute, little ass."

Bradley bit his trembling, lipstick smeared lip as he stared at that pretty, slutty face. "Do you really think so?" he asked.

"Oh yes," Tanya purred. "Everyone would love to pay attention to pretty, little Bridgett. You'd know that if you didn't hide her in the bedroom all the time."

Bridgett whimpered, clutching the edge of the dresser as Tanya worked the fat make-shift dildo under his panties and pressed it against his tight asshole. Bridgett arched his back, making his tender hole more accessible as he looked at his sexy, feminine face.

Tanya began to press the lubricated candle forward. Bridgett stared at the pain in his own expression as his asshole stretched around the girth of the candle. There was a shocked look of violation in his eyes, as if some part of him still couldn't accept what he'd become. His asshole clung to the girth of the candle as it pushed past the resistance of his opening and began to slide into the warm softness of his tender rectum.

"Oh Sweetie," Tanya purred. "You've done this before."

Bridgett didn't answer, but he squeaked with a hint of pain as he arched his narrow back more and pushed his small ass backward, swallowing more of the candle with his quivering rectum.

Tanya smiled. Why had she never done this to a boy before? It was an absolutely delicious feeling. She loved the weak, shivering of the boy, moving across the surface of her tool. She loved the soft little noise he made as she pushed it deeper.

"You're right to dress up," she said as he whimpered, trembling while the make-shift dildo invaded his rectum. "As a boy you are boring. You were probably the most boring and uninteresting person I've ever met... but as a girl..." She tightened her grip on the candle and suddenly plunged it deep inside him. She watched as his mouth shot open and he hissed with surprise. He whimpered with pain and ecstasy as she began to stir the toy inside him. She wiggled it up and down and back and forth, she worked it in small circles, grinding his tender insides from every angle.

She began to roll the candle back, the flesh of his asshole stretched around its girth as it slowly withdrew. "As a girl... well, you're a filthy little whore, but at least your interesting."

"I feel so ashamed," he whimpered, then began to moan as Tanya pushed the candle forward again.

"Good," Tanya said. "I like you to feel ashamed. The world is full of losers with false confidence. It's nice to meet someone who knows what a filthy piece of garbage she really is."

Bridgett bit his lip as the dildo began to withdraw once more.

Tanya pushed the toy forward again, her pussy tingling at the weak little sounds that escaped from the teens lips as she violated his ass. She couldn't resist reaching around him with her free hand and feeling his panties. She let her hands travel to his crotch, caressing the massive bulge in them. As she worked the candle back and forth in his sphincter, she reached into his panties and wrapped her fingers around his throbbing erection. He had a beautiful dick for such a weak and needy boy, and she loved the feeling of its heat and youthful power as she squeezed it in her palm.

As she slid the toy through the tender flesh of his rectum, plunging it back and forth with more speed and power, she also began to slide her soft hand along the length of his pole, gently caressing his throbbing erection.

"You belong to me now, Slut," she purred into the boy's ear. "I claim you as my property, from now until the end of time."

"Thank you," he moaned, his dick throbbing in her hand and his asshole stretched around the tool she worked back and forth inside him.

Tanya began working the makeshift cock faster, the wet sound of her plunging the toy back and forth in his tight asshole filling the room. Bridgett clutched the edge of the dresser, whimpering deliciously as the candle hammered his tender bowels, and Tanya's skilled hands moved across the pulsating flesh of his erection. Tanya's hot breath tickled the back of the boy's neck and earlobe, making all his hairless flesh form goosebumps. He bit his lip in a naturally feminine gesture, working his hips slightly as he was pegged on one side and stroked on the other.

Tanya moved even closer, letting the soft mounds of her gorgeous tits press against his slender back as she plunged the candle harder back and forth.

"Yes," Bridgett moaned. "Yes. Thank you miss. Thank you so much."

"I enjoy it," Tanya purred. "I enjoy what a broken little bitch you are. I love claiming your weak, sissy soul. You belong to me. You're mine."

Bridgett cried out as his body began trembling. "Yes," he whimpered. "Yes. I love you. I worship you. Thank you!" He let out a high-pitched whimper as he began to cum, shooting spurts of creamy jizz against his dresser. His whole body was quivering as he orgasmed from his prostate and his cock at once.

Tanya kissed the back of his long, slender neck, teasing his soft skin with the tip of her tongue as she slowed the pace of her toy. "That's my girl," she said. "Let it all out. Get it all out."

"I love you," Bradley cried as the last jets of cum emptied from his balls. "I love you so much."

The boy had just met her, but Tanya was used to having wild statements of devotion made by needy men. She released his spent dick, letting it snap back against his tummy with the pressure of his panties. She wiped her hand on his shirt, removing the lubricant and the slight spattering of sperm.

Bradley panted as he clutched onto the edge of the dresser, his load splattered against the drawers and dripping down onto the floor. Tanya pulled the candle from his ass and dropped it to the floor for him to clean up. She pinched his cute little ass and purred into his ear, "That's a good little sissy pervert."

He whimpered. "Do you really claim me? Do I really belong to you?" he asked with adorably needy desperation.

"Yes," she purred. "No one will ever touch you like me. No one will ever own the depths of your weakness like I do. You will belong to me long after I'm gone. Long after I get bored of playing with you, I will still dominate your every dream."

"I'll do anything you want. I promise you won't get bored of me."

"That's sweet," Tanya said. "But I bore very easily." She reached under his blouse and teased his hard nipple as her breath washed across his neck and ear. "Tell me; have you ever been hypnotized?"

Bridgett shook his head 'no'.

"I've been developing a few techniques that I'm going to enjoy trying out on you. There are quite a few ideas I have, in fact, that I'm going to enjoy subjecting you to."

"I want it," Bridgett said. "I want it all."

She kissed his ear and turned to stroll away. He turned to face her as she reached his bedroom door. "Can I... Can you still show me your tits?"

Tanya laughed. “Brave now, aren’t you Princess?” She looked at the disheveled boy she had just been playing with, makeup ruined, and skirt splattered with cum. She had found the perfect balance in him between her love of girls and her joy at the weakness and malleability of boys. “Maybe someday, when you earn it.”

He nodded with disappointment, even as he shined with hope.

“What took you so long?” Mr. Branson asked when she joined him on the veranda.

“A gentleman doesn’t complain,” she reminded him. “Anyway. I was thinking of your problem with your son. Perhaps he just needs to get out of the nest and get a job. I have a few new ideas for my resort that he might be very helpful with. I’ll be taking him with me when I leave.”

“But he has school,” the man pointed out.

“Don’t worry about that,” Tanya purred. “I’ll teach him everything he needs to know.”

Hitching the Road to Freedom

"Where are we going?" the sexy little Asian tranny purred.

"Wherever," Heather answered. "Anywhere we can get a ride to." Heather was wearing a skin-tight white t shirt and denim shorts she had shoplifted from the store. The faded jean shorts weren't intended for someone so tall, and they barely covered the curve of her delicate ass-cheeks. All three of the lustrous shemales wore flip-flop sandals and carried their supplies in little, stuffed animal backpacks. They wore stolen truck-stop t shirts and pre-faded denim shorts. Heather extended her slender, pale arm and raised her thumb, smiling in the direction the cars would be coming from.

Ting looked out at the sparse back-highway traffic. The pink t shirt she wore stretched over her big, fake tits said, "Daddy's girl" and the ballcap she had on said "Trucker." She looked skeptically out at the traffic. "What if we get picked up by..." she stopped speaking. Her time of being brainwashed into living out other men's fantasies left her with a mind that couldn't imagine any situation that wouldn't end in filthy and fulfilling sex.

Jen followed along behind them, a blank and brainless look on her beautiful face. Her strappy tank-top was blue, and printed across with big silver letters, distorted by her impressive rack, was the statement, "Wish you were Beer." The shirt ended just at the base of her delicate ribcage showing off the sexy blonde's slinky torso.

The first vehicle to pass them was an older black van. It passed them by a foot then skidded to a jarring, crooked stop, tires squealing and smoking as it almost slid off the road. The passenger door swung open and a man leaned out from the driver's seat, waving his arm.

"You girl's need a ride?" he called out in a voice that strained with frantic hope and disbelief.

Heather smiled back at Ting then began strolling towards the van on her impossibly long legs. Ting took Jen by the hand and they began walking behind the waifish redhead. The lushly curved Asian and model perfect blonde walked hand in hand, their arms swinging girlishly between them.

The girls all crowded into the car, Heather allowed the two other girls to squeeze in first and move to the back, then she sat in the passenger seat, smiling beautifully at a middle-aged man.

Dexter Atwood was a forty-year old factory worker who had just been laid off. His house had recently been foreclosed and his meager possessions all shoved in the back of his van. He slept back there on his long drive across the country, hoping to find work. He stared at the three girls who crowded into his van now. Each one of them was more stunning than any woman he'd ever met. They all had the flawless look of movie stars and the grace to match it. There was a sensual quality to each of them, from the way they held their slender bodies to the slinky way they moved.

"Hi," he said. "Where you girls headed?" Wherever it was, that's where he was headed too. He was certain of that.

The redhead purred. "I'm Heather." She pointed out her friends and introduced them as well. "Were going anywhere you want to take us."

Dexter sat for a long moment with his mouth hanging open. This was clearly some kind of joke. Either that or… "I'm embarrassed to say," he said. "But if you girls are some kind of professionals, there's no way I can afford any one of you."

Heather wasn't sure what he meant. She could remember being many kinds of professionals during her time at the dollhouse. She had been a delivery girl, a plumber, a nurse; she had been a CIA interrogator and an angry, corrupt police-girl; she had been cheerleaders and schoolteachers and cocktail waitresses desperate for tips. She reached out and touched his arm. "We can be whatever you want," she said. "Just please take us as far from here as you can."

The man nodded, twisted the wheel and stepped on the gas. A moment later they were speeding down the highway once more. It was an older model van, with a rough suspension. They could feel every bump in the highway and hear every mile roaring as the massive engine propelled them forward.

The car sped down the road for a while, then Jen began sighing as if she was uncomfortable or bored.

"What is it?" Ting finally asked her.

"I'm horny," Jen complained in a high, whimpering voice. "How long has it been since I've been fucked?"

Ting looked at her watch. "Three hours, Sweetie."

Heather wanted to laugh at the little blonde, but she could feel it too. Deep in her slender, sissy bones, she craved the rough hands of a man on her hormone-filled body. Perhaps it was being in this state of awareness, instead of being put into a hypnotic and mindless state when she wasn't being used, but she felt a deep hunger for ecstasy pulsating within her, making her tingle from her pink nipples to her hairless balls to her delicate painted toes. She looked at Ting and knew the little Asian felt it too. All them were burning with intensifying and unquenchable urges.

She looked over at the driver. He was nervous and sweating. In spite of Jen's words, which seemed like a clear invitation, he hadn't responded. He clutched the wheel, staring straight down the road as if the road was packed with traffic instead of nearly abandoned. Heather decided it was time to take matters into her own hand. She turned her body so her long, skinny legs filled the space between the driver's and passenger seat. She leaned over them, her slim torso elongating as she stretched forward, purring. She extended the long, pale fingers of one hand forward, running softly over his jeans.

His voice was full of terrified desire as he said, "What are you doing?"

"You seem stressed," Heather purred, running her hand across his thigh to his crotch. His bugle instantly began to swell, beneath the denim. Her hand squeezed gently around the imprint of his hardening meat. "I used to be a masseuse you know."

She moved forward, dropping to her knees between the seats, her hands still cupping his package. She could feel the vibrations of the engine through her knees as the van continued thundering down the highway. She moved higher on her knees, her red hair streaming as she wiggled her head into the space between his leg and his arm.

Dexter made space for her, his breathing deepening. He looked in the rear-view mirror and saw that the voluptuous little Asian and the supple blonde had begun to kiss. Their luscious lips were pressed together, pink tongues darting in and out of each other's mouths as their small, perfect hands began frantically clutching each other's dramatic curves. He watched them begin to wiggle out of their tops as he heard the sound of his zipper being opened by the slinky redhead. He looked down at the fiery red hair draped over his lap, the girl's thin back stretching to her petite ass. She knelt on her insanely long legs as she pulled his erection out of his pants.

He reached down and with his fingertips, tentatively touched her soft, pale skin, imagining she might disappear like a dream any minute. But suddenly, the sensation of her small, wet mouth wrapping around his throbbing hardon made him shudder and realize that this was really happening.

"Oh fuck," he moaned. "Oh, fuck yes."

Her red hair tossed and tousled in waves as her head began to bob up and down on his throbbing prick. He didn't think he'd ever been this hard before. He caressed her soft locks of fiery hair.

The intense suction of her amazing mouth made his toes curl. In all his life he'd never been sucked as expertly or with as much enthusiasm. He let out a deep moan as every muscle in his body seemed to relax at once, losing all his concerns into the wet cavern of her young, pretty mouth.

He looked up and realized he was drifting out of his lane. "Shit," he groaned, correcting the van's path. He spotted a gravel shoulder and began to slow the van as he pulled towards it. Glancing in the rearview mirror he saw the blonde and the Asian, their naked tits rubbing together as their pink tongue flickered and pulsed past each other's luscious lips.

Heather's lips continued to cradle his meat, rising and falling along his shaft as he brought the van to a stop by the side of the road. The girls in the back, naked except for skimpy denim shorts seemed oblivious of everything except each other. Their hands moved frantically across each other's supple flesh as they kissed with wild, passionate intensity.

Dexter looked back and forth from the beautiful girls kissing in his rearview mirror to the stunning redhead slobbering up and down his pole. His cock was harder than it had ever been in his life. The sloppy noises of Heather's mouth slurping and slobbering on him pushed him close to the edge, but he took a deep breath, wanting to prolong this moment as long as possible.

In the rearview mirror, the two girls began to work at the buttons of each other's skimpy shorts, pulling them open with agile fingers as they continued to explore each other's mouths with eager tongues. Dexter licked his lips, watching as those shorts pulled open to reveal the sexy lace of panties. The girl's hands slid under the panties, reaching into each other's crotches.

The girls kissing wetly and the redhead sucking him rhythmically, he waited eagerly for a glimpse at the two young girls' pussies. He watched with expectation as the blonde and the Asian each pulled the other's panties down enough to reveal what looked like two, very small, fully erect penises.

Dexter stared, waiting for the illusion to pass. His mind spun, trying to make out what those two little rods really were. The two girls continued kissing, wiggling their bodies together, pink nipples rubbing against pink nipples, their fingers pinching each other's mysterious little pole. The shocking realization sunk in as he watched the girls stroking each other's small hardon, their fingers moving up and down in a steady, even pace as their free hands squeezed ass or tits and their tongues writhed and wiggled together. Those girls really did have dicks.

Dexter gasped in deep, soul shaking shock, a wet mouth continuing to move up and down his throbbing prick.

He looked down at the redhead, his whole body frozen. "Wait," he said. "Wait. Wait!"

She looked up from his cock, a patient look on her flawless, feminine face. Her graceful hand continued to slide up and down his spit-wet dick, caressing him with expert pressure as she gazed up at him, smiling.

"Are you..." he stumbled over his words. How do you accuse one of the most beautiful women you've ever seen of not actually being a woman? He looked in the rear-view mirror, where the other two most beautiful women he'd ever seen stroked each other's cocks as they plunged their tongues into each other's mouths, perfect tits pressing together. He looked at Heather once more. "Do you have a... do you have a dick?"

She smiled as if it was the most natural question in the world. "Of course. Do you want to see it?"

He didn't want to see it. It was like driving past the scene of a shocking accident. He shook his head, but the word that came out of his mouth was, "Yes."

Heather leaned back, releasing his cock. She pulled off her t shirt, exposing her perky breasts, pink nipples hard and glistening. Her slender torso looked fragile and feminine, her skin pale and freckled. She began unbuttoning her tiny faded-jean shorts.

She opened the shorts, revealing the pink lace of her panties. She reached in her shorts and pulled out a big, limp, hairless pink dick. She brought one hand to her mouth and licked her thumb, then she wrapped that hand around her shaft, rubbing the tip with her saliva coated thumb.

If this was the internet Dexter would have laughed and said it was photoshop, but right here in front of him, he watched the most stunningly feminine woman he'd ever seen, make her big cock get hard in her graceful hand. The tip was pink and bulging, the swollen flesh glistening with saliva.

She was much bigger than him. He glanced back in the mirror again. The two other girls were sprawled out on the van's floor, completely naked now, sucking each other in the sixty-nine position. He looked at Heather once more. "What are you?" he asked.

"What do you want me to be?" was her playful reply.

He looked down her long body. Her luscious young skin pale and radiating in the sunlight, her perky breasts tall with lovely pink nipples, her vivid red hair in frantic disarray, her beautiful face, long slender legs, her slutty shorts pulled down just enough to let her big, throbbing cock free. Something deep in his perspective of the universe spun one-hundred and eighty degrees.

"You're fucking perfect," he said.

"That's sweet," she said. "Can I finish blowing you now? I'm so hungry for your cum, Daddy."

"Oh fuck," Dexter moaned. "I can't believe this is really happening."

Heather smiled teasingly, and she leaned forward, one hand still wrapped around her own cock, the other hand wrapping around his. She looked into his eyes as she stroked them both in unison. She moaned softly, her whole-body swaying with pleasure as she squeezed her hand up and down both erections. Dexter looked at her hand on his fat, throbbing cock, then he looked at her hand on her own. There was something pretty about that pink dick. In spite of its size, it seemed almost feminine; perfectly straight and balanced, flawlessly clean and cared for, tip glistening with saliva.

"I love the contrast," she said as her hands rolled up and down both dicks at once. "Do you want to feel?"

Again, he couldn't fight the word that came out. "Yes," he said.

Heather released her own cock and reached up, taking Dexter's hand. She pulled Dexter's reluctant hand gently down till it was resting against the hot flesh of her throbbing hardon. She rubbed his hand against it, feeling the smooth contours of her meat. Finally, Dexter surrendered and took her in his grasp.

Dexter stroked her as she stroked him, their hands moving in perfect unison. Her dick felt incredibly different from his own. Where his was crocked and bulging and almost monstrous, hers was flawlessly formed, perfectly symmetrical and deliciously pink.

Heather leaned forward, dropping her head over his lap once more. Her hand continued to mirror his, rising and falling along the length of his pole, but now her lips began to follow, sliding along the length of his meat, creating a trail of glistening drool.

Dexter moaned, losing himself in the sensation of wet mouth and fingers moving up and down his prick, as his own hand squeezed the hot, rigid flesh of the shemale's beautiful dick. Glancing in the mirror he watched the girls in the back. Their lustrous, bimbo lips were sliding up and down each other's small dicks. They each were pressing two fingers into the other's smooth, pretty asshole. He watched their luscious little bodies writhing against each other, their luminous hair draping over each other's slender thighs and tickling their tiny hairless balls as their lips moved up and down and their fingers moved in and out.

He looked down at the redhead, her head was bobbing faster as her hand squeezed tighter, jerking up and down his shaft. He began jerking her faster as well, feeling the powerful pulsations of her cock as he rubbed it with his clumsy hand.

Her whole-body began to bounce over him as she grew more enthusiastic. His body began to move as well; rocking and twitching as her hand, mouth and torso rose and fell above him as one unit, filling him with uncontrollable ecstasy. He felt like a bucking bronco, being ridden by a very naughty cowgirl as his whole body began to pulsate. His hand continued to slide up and down her erection, but he couldn't keep up with her rhythm as her mouth and hand pumped him frantically.

"Yes," he groaned. "Oh, fuck yes!"

Heather responded with even more intensity. Her body rising and falling, mouth and hand slamming against him without regard for her own, delicate flesh or the tightness of her own narrow throat.

"Fuck!" Dexter cried. He lost all sense of where he was as his legs jerked rigid, his balls tightened, and he began to spray his sperm into the gorgeous redhead's mouth. Heather continued jerking and sucking, pumping every drop of cum out of him and swallowing it down. Finally, when every drop had been milked from his balls, she leaned back. She placed her hands on the floor behind her, arching her back and creating a beautiful curved line from her perfect tits to her throbbing hardon.

Dexter had been barely stroking her as his ecstasy took over, but now he began to focus on her again. He stroked the girl frantically, staring at her beautiful face. He watched the expressions of pleasure moving across her feminine features, her fiery red hair streaking across her reddish flesh. She began to moan, her tits rising and torso elongating with each movement of his hand.

"Yes," Heather purred. "Oh yes. Stroke me, Daddy. Make me cum."

Dexter jerked her frantically, watching her pert tits move, staring at her luscious red lips and long, slender neck. He squeezed down on the big, pink cock that poked out of her slutty little shorts.

"Yes," she purred. "Oh yes Daddy. I love it. I love it."

He could see her slinky body beginning to tremble, her eyes closed, her lips parted.

"Yes," she cried out as she began to climax. She exploded like a bomb, her first wad of cum splattering against the roof of the van.

Dexter continued jerking her, pointing her cock closer to her body. Her second shot of jizz hit her in a long string across her cheek and lips. Another glazed one of her pale breasts. Dexter continued jacking her, watching her spray glistening semen all over her own, supple, freckled skin.

When she finished cumming she smiled up at him, a streak of semen slashed across her face like a scar. "Thanks Daddy," she said.

Suddenly the other two girls were squeezing into the front, pressing themselves against the redhead and licking up the cum that had been sprayed across her long, slim body, and pretty, pale face. Heather giggled as the other two girls lapped at her like kittens, wrapping her arms around them.

Dexter watched the three feminine bodies wiggling together for a minute, then he closed his jeans, and started the van once more. He was going to drive these girls anywhere they wanted to go, because that's where he wanted to go too.

Tranny Pet

Back before Tanya's island was a forced feminization compound, back when it was just a resort for desperate, female prostitutes to service wealthy men, Bridgett was Tanya Payne's only doll. The first time Bridgett flew to the island he did it curled up on a little pet-mattress in the corner of Tanya's private plane. The eighteen-year-old crossdresser had spent weeks getting hypnotized and drugged by his beloved new mistress. She toyed with his thoughts and beliefs merely out of curiosity, with no particular plan or strategy. She seemed to savor the long hours she spent with him, twisting his needy mind. One minute she would convince him he really was the girl he'd always secretly longed to be, then the next minute she would convince him he was a furry little dog.

Bridgett, for his own part, knew that these things were not true. Except, on a deeper level, he also knew they were true. Tanya told him stories, painting pictures in his mind as he lay in a hypnotic state, and he knew she was just whispering these ideas in his mind, playing with his thoughts like a cat plays with a stunned mouse; but as he looked at each thing she whispered into his brain, he noticed that each one also happened to be true. Now he lay in his padded pink training bra, stockings and heels, his cute lace pink panties pulled aside and a butt-plug in his ass. The butt-plug had a long black extension that seemed to form a lustrous, shimmering tail out of his tight, feminine ass.

Bridgett wasn't really a dog. But on some deeper, more meaningful level that was beyond truth, and more important than mere fact, he had always been a dog. He had always been a dog, dreaming of being Tanya Payne's loyal little pet.

He lay on his pet mattress, his long hair soft and dark and draped across his slender, feminine neck. His young flesh looked even more vivid and feminine from the natural hormones that the feminizing hypnosis was releasing in him, as well as the synthetic hormones that Tanya Payne had begun injecting into him.

He couldn't remember if she ever asked his permission for any of these things, but he didn't suppose it mattered. If she wanted his permission all she had to do was command him to give it to her.

He arched his back and looked up when he heard Tanya purr, "Oh doggie."

Two generic looking blonde bimbo whores shared the flight with them. They were giggling as Tanya slapped her gorgeous knee, calling him forward. Tanya looked magnificent and shapely in a well fitted, and sophisticated looking dress, her long legs revealed as the long slit up the dress allowed it to fall open. Bridgett hopped to his hands and knees and began to crawl towards his beautiful mistress. The two bitches were giggling and whispering into each other's ears in the seats along the far side of the private plane.

Bridgett felt sexier and more beautiful than he ever imagined possible. He pressed his pretty, makeup covered face against the side of Tanya's perfectly formed calf and purred. He shook his ass to make his tail wag, the butt plug wiggling inside him.

Tanya reached down with one hand and gently caressed his neck, filling him with shuddering pleasure. The girls laughed at his needy soul as he rubbed his soft, pretty face against the lustrous flesh of Tanya's leg.

"Good doggie," Tanya purred, her voice making Bridgett shudder with pleasure. Her sensual voice reverberated with incredible power, seeming to automatically reach into Bridgett's brain and begin touching things, caressing the connections between ideas and thoughts. It was amazing how the sound of this woman's voice could give him more pleasure then any touch he'd known.

"It's a good thing you are such a good doggie," Tanya said. "Because you're worthless a man." Tanya purring voice made the state of his pathetic weakness sound delicious. Indeed, it was delicious.

He was a deliciously helpless thing. If he could provide his mistress one moment of amusement he would be of more use than he had ever been in his entire life. He breathed deep, his eyelids fluttering. "I am worthless," he said.

"You are weak, and you are nothing. You have no power or value... except..."

That one possible exception hung in the air like a teasing promise, floating above Bridgett's young, feminine body. "Except." The word had a terrifying implication of power.

Tanya continued. "You belong to me. You belong to me and I have power. My beauty and my perfection are powerful. My strength and my superior intellect give me power. My pussy, hot and wet between my slender thighs is more powerful than every ounce of your pathetic will. But because I am truly powerful, I can give you a little of my power. I can grant you a little taste of my unlimited beauty and power. I can unleash you, my obedient little pet, on anyone. I know that my pet will be strong. You can face anyone I command, because it is not the worthless dog that you are that faces them, but a tiny sliver of the beautiful goddess that I am."

Bridgett swam in excitement, wanting to taste that flawless, feminine power. He bowed his head, kissing his mistress's gorgeous feet. He could hear the two beautiful bimbos laughing but he didn't care. They had hot, wet pussies between their lovely long legs as well, but they would never have the same power as Tanya Payne. He could endure any humiliation to taste his lovely goddess's power.

"Stand up, doll," Tanya said. "Show me how elegant and pretty you can be."

As Bridgett rose, Tanya reached around him and pulled the butt-plug tail from his ass. She let it drop to the floor and then she adjusted Bridgett's panties.

"You are no longer my puppy-dog," Tanya purred. "You are an extension of my power. You are my punishing hand, unleashed on the world."

All Bridgette's years of practice, dressed up in front of his own bedroom mirror, practicing walking and posing, paid off now, as he stood and smiled beautifully, slender body lithe and young, his supple movements giving him the appearance of delicious curves.

"Good girl," Tanya said. "That's my good, pretty girl."

The bimbos were laughing at him, whispering to each other.

"And for being such a good, pretty girl for me," Tanya said. "And for being such an obedient instrument of my power, I have a present for you. For the next two hours, I give you both these girls. You can do anything you want with them, or make them do anything you want to you or to each other."

The bimbos stopped laughing. "Wait... What?" The tall one asked.

Tanya looked back at them, acknowledging them for the first time. "You did say you would do anything for the job. Did you imagine I wouldn't collect on that promise?"

The girls both looked down at their slim, tan knees. Their heavily made-up, doll-like faces barely showed expression as they nodded with reluctant submission. Bridgette felt his body coming alive, his dick stirring inside his panties. The two luscious little blondes were curvaceous and radiant. They reminded him of all those perfect girls at school who wouldn't even talk to him. Bridgett smiled and strolled forward, feeling confident, imagining Tanya's glorious power moving inside him. He channeled every vicious soap-opera vixen he'd ever studied as he said, "Strip."

The girl's looked from Bridgett to Ms. Payne, and when Tanya didn't offer them a way out, they looked at each other.

"Now," Bridgette said. "Otherwise it's the belt." Bridgette smiled as they began to comply. He had already decided they were getting the belt either way. He had a gorgeous red leather belt in his bag that would deliciously complement the girls' youthful tan skin as it slashed across their supple bodies.

The girls both stood up and began stripping out of their clothes. They had a resigned businesslike attitude. Whatever reluctance they felt had been put aside as they got on with the job of whoring. Bridgett went to his bag and got out the long, leather belt. It was thin and tapering, with floral imprints weaved into the leather. He ran it through his feminine hand, feeling the ridges of the imprint before he folded it over itself and snapped it into the air. He turned and walked back to the girls. They had luscious, curved bodies and vibrant skin, their tits too big for their slim frames. One was tall, about 5'9" and the other was as short as Bridgett, standing at 5'3".

"Turn around," Bridgett ordered. He could feel Tanya's eyes on him, appraising his demeanor and command. He tried to be worthy of the tiny piece of herself he had been given as he snapped the belt through the air and whipped the tall ones lush, curving ass.

The girl squealed as the leather touched her flesh, a thin red line painted across her perky, young ass-cheek. Bridgett licked his glossy red lips as he watched the flesh of the girl's ass jiggle from the impact. He saw the other girl tense in anticipation and decided to keep her waiting as he once again slashed his belt across the tall one's ass. The short one flinched as if it was her being struck and the tall one hissed with the sting of the blow.

Bridgett tried not to look back at Tanya, but he could see her moving out of the corner of his eye. Tanya changed her position to watch the show. He could feel as well as see his gorgeous mistress spreading her impossibly long legs, caressing them with her graceful fingertips.

Bridgett whipped the tall girl again, the sound of the leather snapping against her luscious ass making him shiver. His big, hard cock was pushing against his panties, stretching them, the lace flowers distorting around his bulging meat.

Tanya's gorgeous dress was split up to her thigh. Her long legs and slender thighs were exposed, skin beautiful and lustrous as her fingertips teased the inside of her thighs.

Bridgett whipped the tall girl again, listening to the sound of the belt and the sound of her whimpers. The short girl was whimpering too, the expectation of her coming punishment making her tremble.

Tanya wore luxurious silk panties, the front adorned with delicate lace. Tanya slid her fingertips underneath them, pressing them to the soft, pink flesh of her amazing pussy.

Bridgett slashed the tall girl across her graceful back, watching the deliciously soft flesh turn red. He could hear Tanya beginning to moan as she rubbed her own flawless cunt with her artistic fingers. He raised the belt again, and this time he brought it down across the short girl's tight, high rump.

The surprised cry of the short one filled the room as Bridgett whipped her luscious little ass once more.

"Comfort each other," Bridgett said. "Touch each other. Kiss each other."

The girls turned towards each other, their luscious bodies touching as they wrapped their arms around each other's slim waists. They watched Bridgett out of the corner of their eyes as they pressed their lips together, kissing without passion.

Bridgett whipped them across their touching thighs. "Mean it," he said. "Make it count."

The girl's extended their tongues, pressing them into each other's wet mouths as their hands began to work frantically over each other's stinging flesh, touching each other. The beautiful young whores were experts at faking enthusiasm, and they began to moan and purr, wriggling their tongues together and lapping up each other's drool.

Bridgett's cock throbbed. He could hear his mistress's luscious voice moaning as she touched her beautiful pussy with her graceful fingers.

The two bimbos continued to grope and kiss each other, their plump red lips mashing together as their hands squeezed lush curves.

Bridgett turned to his mistress. "What do you want me to do with them now?" he asked.

"Whatever you want, Pet," she said. "Obedience does have some rewards."

Bridgett turned towards the two beautiful blondes. How many times had he dreamed of girls like this touching him or being touched by him. His entire body was alive with heat and electricity. His nipples hard against the soft training bra he wore, his hard cock ruining his pretty panties. "Get on your knees," he said. "Get on your knees and open your dumb, bimbo mouths."

They did not laugh at him anymore. The dropped to their knees like they had many times for money or attention. Their bodies pressed together as they knelt side by side, licking their lips and waiting. Bridgett pulled down his panties and stepped closer. The girls did not react with revulsion, they simply waited, ready to do what was required.

Bridgett hesitated. The idea of actually having his dick in a woman's mouth seemed like an impossible dream and he had given up on it years ago, but now there were not one, but two beautiful girls, eager for money and whipped into compliance, perfectly willing to suck him off. He wasn't sure if he could go through with it. He wasn't worthy of them. He didn't deserve the pleasure of their beautiful young mouths. He realized he was shaking.

Tanya purred, her hand moving beneath her panties. The two girls waited on their knees, ready to do what they were told, their plump red lips glistening.

"Give it to them," Tanya purred. "You have my permission to play with my toys. You have my permission to feel pleasure. You are a worthless thing, but you are my worthless thing, and I want to watch you cum."

Bridgett finally surrendered to the need pulsating inside him. He pulled his panties down enough to release his big, throbbing hardon. The girls didn't hesitate to lean forward and press their lush red lips to either side of his bulging, pink tip. Their tongues darted out of their mouths and lapped at his bulging contours. They began to slather him in saliva as they worked their way up and down either side of his pole.

Bridgett bit his lip and whimpered. His small, tight feminine frame was rocking side to side as the sensation of two wet mouths overwhelmed his senses.

"That's my pretty girl," Tanya purred, her voice raising in pitch as her fingers worked beneath her panties. "That's my beautiful little pet. Use those little whores. Use those little whore mouths."

Bridgett began to rock his hips, driving his cock back and forth between the girls' mouths, their slick, wet lips pressing against his cock. Their tongues continued to caress around his pole, dancing along his meat and brushing against each other as his dick was jacked by the friction of their mouths. Blonde hair spilled across his smooth thighs and tickled his thin, feminine legs as his dick throbbed and pulsated with pleasure and heat. The tall girl brought her lips up to his tip, then stretched them open and allowed his straining erection to press into her wet mouth.

Bridgett gasped as he felt his raging hardon submerged in the soft flesh and saliva of the bimbo's willing orifice. He whimpered in his feminine voice, still not believing he could be allowed to experience this thrill.

The short girl began pulling his pretty pink panties down lower. She licked a path that followed his dropping panties, lapping from his shaft to his slick, shaved balls, teasing them with the tip of her soft, spongy tongue.

The belt slipped from Bridgett's hand as he forgot about it. He brought his palms to the back of each girl's head, feeling their luxurious hair. The tall one began to slide her lips down Bridgett's thick, throbbing shaft as the short one continued to lap at his hairless balls and slender thighs. The two girls fell into a rhythm. The short one kissing low on Bridgett's balls as the tall one's lips moved down his shaft. The short one's wet tongue began moving up and she began to kiss higher up the base of his pole as the tall one brought her glossy red lips to the very tip of his dick.

The two lustrous bimbos repeated the motion, licking up and down his balls and sucking up and down his throbbing prick.

Bridgett whimpered as the rhythm grew steady and then began to increase in speed. His pretty, painted toenails curled as he closed his eyes, losing himself in the sensation of the sexy girls' mouths, and in the sensation of his own, sensual body, soft and tingling with beautiful feminine energy.

Tanya rubbed herself faster as she watched the two girls kneeling in front of the lithe, young crossdresser. They worked like the expert whores they were, forgetting the reluctant beating they had accepted as they worked in harmony to suck cock.

Bridgett looked stunning, in full makeup, a sexy training bra, his delicate panties pulled down his thin, deliciously tan legs. His beautiful eyes were closed and his painted lips parted as he moaned in ecstasy. The tall girl let Bridgett's cock slip from between her lips and the short one pressed it between hers and continued sucking without a beat being missed.

The two blondes were beautiful and skilled little whores, and they looked sexy slobbering on Bridgett's dick, but Tanya's eyes kept being drawn back to the slinky little crossdresser. Tanya suddenly realized two things: First, with continued hormones and a few minor cosmetic surgeries, Bridgett would be more beautiful than either one of these girls ever had the potential of being. The other thing she realized was: while the girls were doing what they needed to do to keep their new job, Bridgett was living out his fantasy, and it showed in his enthusiasm and energy. Tanya didn't need an army of pretty hookers she could manipulate and exploit, she needed an army of sissy boys with weak, needy little minds, that she could tell what to fantasize about.

The girls took turns sucking on Bridgett's throbbing erection, their beautiful young faces side by side. First one pair of lips, then the other, wrapping around Bridgett's meat without losing a stroke. Bridgett's narrow, defined ribcage rose and fell as his breathing deepened, his training bra pushing out from his slender chest like a waifish girl's tiny rack as he whimpered and moaned with pleasure.

As Bridgett's breathing grew deeper and faster, the girls began to lick him instead of sucking him, working their tongues across his pulsating meat like they were sharing an ice cream. The tall one squeezed his shaft in her fist and began to jerk him as they licked, his dick slapping back and forth between their glistening, drool covered lips.

"Yes," Bridgett whimpered, his long dark hair trickling across his narrow, tan back. "Yes."

Tanya bit her lip as she worked her clit faster, watching the pleasure she was allowing her weak little crossdressing pet to enjoy.

"Yes," Bridgett continued to cry in his feminine voice, his slim hips pumping as he was jacked between two slippery wet tongues. "Oh shit."

Tanya breathed in as her body began to tingle with pleasure, energy jolting out from her pussy as she experienced a small but thrilling orgasm.

Bridgett cried out as he too began to orgasm, but his orgasm was all consuming. His delicate, feminized body shuddered and stumbled as he began to spray hot jizz like a firehose. Wads of thick cream splattered against the beautiful bimbo's faces, and into their radiant blonde hair as they continued to kiss in front of his meat, jacking him relentlessly. As Bridgett stumbled backwards, his cum slick dick slipped from the tall one's grip and he collapsed onto his tight little ass onto the floor. The girls didn't look at him sprawled out there, but continued to kiss each other, cleaning each other's faces with their tongues.

Tanya stood up and adjusted her dress. She walked up to Bridgett and held out her hand, "Come here, Pet."

Bridgett looked up at her with utter devotion as he fixed his panties, rose to his feet and took her hand. Tanya looked over at the girls who were just finishing licking the cum from each other's faces. Tanya smiled and told them, "I changed my mind. You filthy little whores stay on the plane. I have no use for you."

The girls knelt on the floor, eyes wide with shock as Tanya took her adorable pet by the hand and led him off the plane.

Tranny Paradise Motel

Jen looked around the motel room. It was basic, with a bed, a table and a small cramped room to the side for a toilet and shower. Ting and Heather were already in the room. Heather was sitting on the bed in her tiny cutoff shorts. She was pressed beside the man who drove the van they'd been riding in for the past few hours. He was a middle-aged man with a nervous demeaner, but he seemed nice. He had been nice enough to stroke Heather's dick in the car. Most guys didn't want to have anything to do with a girl's dick, so Jen always appreciated it when they did.

Ting was already stripping for a shower. Jen and the man, Dexter was his name, were both staring at Ting's supple, caramel colored flesh as the beautiful Asian uncovered her dramatically curved frame. Her magnificent pink-tipped tits barely moved as she pulled off her thong and stepped towards the bathroom, her tiny dick poking out in front of her. Jen noticed Dexter stare for a moment, then look away from the tiny rod and small, hairless balls.

He was shy, Jen realized. It was cute. Perhaps he was too shy and nervous to touch another one of their dicks, but Jen didn't care about that. Jen only cared about the man's dick, or even Heather's dick. Jen needed to feel a big cock, hard and throbbing, stuffing into either of his soft, hungry holes. Jen smiled a tantalizing smile at the empty air and began to strip out of his top.

Heather and the man were both watching as Jen exposed his gorgeous, artificial breasts. Jen pretended to be oblivious, stretching his lithe little body with model-like poise, not looking back at them as they both inspected his lavish curves and soft, feminine skin. Jen stripped down to nothing but panties, then turned his practiced smile on the man. "You don't mind if I get comfy, do you?" Jen asked.

The man's eyes were locked on the large, firm breasts pushing out from Jen's narrow torso. He swallowed and shook his head no. Heather was looking at Jen's sexy little body too, her own deliciously feminized frame pressed against the man as her hand caressed up and down his thigh, touching him through the fabric. Heather's t shirt clung to her slinky body, ripe little tits pushing against the cotton. Jen could see the man's cock beginning to bulge in his slacks.

Jen couldn't remember where they were, or how exactly he'd gotten there, but for some time he had been fighting a terrible feeling of being lost. But that feeling was evaporating as he began to sway enticingly in front of an audience. Jen was finally doing what he was meant to once more. He finally had a purpose again. Jen knew that the other luscious trannies he traveled with were looking for something, but Jen already knew what he was. He was born and built and born again to be shiny little fuck-thing. It was his highest and onlyest desire.

Jen's slinky, curved body writhed gently as if he was swaying to some music that only the model-perfect shemale could hear. He could feel the attention of the man and the tall, waifish redhead beside him. Jen ran his hands down his flat tummy, then up along his full, rounded hips. He drew them up the bones of his delicate ribcage and brought them to his full, luscious tits. He cupped his tits, squeezing them, letting his luscious lips slip open. He closed his eyes, flicking his wet tongue across his glossy-red, hormone softened lips. "Mmmmm," Jen purred.

Jen could feel the stares, even without looking at the two figures on the bed. The heat of their attention made Jen's flesh tingle, his tiny prick growing inside his tight little panties. Jen covered it with one hand, his other hand still cupping one of his luscious tits. Jen felt his little erection throbbing against his palm as he covered the bulge in his panties. He pressed his palm firmly against the silky fabric of his panties and began to apply friction. His fingers riding the soft fabric of his panties, pointing down at the space between his tiny balls and his tight asshole, he rubbed his hand up and down, jacking himself inside his sexy underwear with the silky palm of one hand.

Heather rose to her feet and peeled off her top. Jen looked at her, licking his lips again as he saw the impossibly slender frame of the tall redhead. Heather stepped closer, flicking open the buttons of her tiny denim shorts. Heather was swaying now too, moving as if she too could hear the music Jen had imagined; peeling the tight little shorts over her deliciously curved hips.

Heather let the shorts fall, so that she was wearing only panties. She kicked the shorts aside and continued to sway gracefully as she moved closer. Jen's own penis throbbed against the flat of his palm as he looked at the redhead's body, at once pixie-like and Amazonian, a massive, semi-erect cock tucked into her pretty, pink panties. Heather circled around behind Jen and pressed her body against his.

Jen could feel the tall redhead's dick against the small of his slender back as her firm tits pressed against his shoulder blades. He looked at the man on the bed. He had his pants down now, pushed to his ankles as he held his fat, curved, vein-crossed cock in his hairy fist. Jen stared at the man and smiled as Heather's hands began to caress the front of his body, feeling his silky, soft feminized skin. One of Heather's hands slid under Jen's panties and she wrapped her fingers around his small, throbbing erection, purring into his ear, "You're so beautiful, Sweetie."

Jen writhed his little frame, curling back against the redhead. Jen reached behind himself and touched Heather's tight, curved ass, squeezing it as Heather squeezed his dick and one of his luscious fake tits. The man was watching carefully, stroking his cock slowly as if wanting to savor the sensation and the view. Jen stared into the man's eyes as Heather's hands caressed his velvety skin. The man stared back into Jen's radiant blue eyes. Jen could see himself reflected in the mirror behind the bed. It turned him on even more to see how hot his surgically enhanced and chemically altered body was. He stood watching the delicious blonde in the mirror getting groped by the tall, slinky redhead.

Jen squeezed Heather's lush little ass as Heather's hard cock pressed against Jen's spine. Jen wanted that hot, throbbing meat to be inside his tight little hole. "Fuck me," Jen begged. "Fuck me with your big, gorgeous cock."

The man licked his lips. "Yes," he moaned, stroking his fat cock faster. "Fuck her. Fuck her with that beautiful tranny dick."

Jen began tugging at Heather's panties, peeling them down as Heather squirmed out of them, her throbbing cock slithering across Jen's smooth flesh. "I want to fuck you so bad," Heather moaned into his ear, twisting one of his hard, pink nipples in her fingertips. "I want to feel the tight flesh of your soft sissy-cunt pressing down on my me."

"Take it," Jen moaned. "Take my sissy-cunt. Please take it."

Heather kicked her panties aside and began to work on peeling Jen's off. She knelt as she pulled Jen's panties to his ankles then waited for him to step each delicate foot out. Still kneeling, Heather grabbed a handful of Jen's beautifully curved ass-cheeks with each hand and pried them apart, exposing his tender, bleached-pink asshole.

"Mmmm," Heather purred, admiring it as she leaned in and pressed her pretty face between Jen's ass-cheeks. Heather gave Jen's ass a tender kiss, then a flick of her tongue.

Jen purred as he felt the cool wetness of Heather's agile tongue beginning to probe and tickle his opening. "Yes," he whimpered. "Oh yes." He moaned as Heather began to explore deeper, penetrating his anus with her tongue and wiggling it inside him.

The man was stroking faster, his voice more and more excited. "Oh yes," he groaned. "Eat that sissy-cunt, girl. Eat that hot little sissy-cunt."

Heather was driving her tongue deep inside of Jen now. Jen whimpered as he felt himself being licked from the inside. Heather's tongue began to slide in and out of his rectum, driving wetly through his opening as the stunning redhead began to tongue-fuck his asshole.

Jen whimpered in his high, feminine voice, rubbing his little erection with the palm of his hand once more. "Yes. Oh yes."

Heather's tongue darted from inside Jen's hole and she ran it up the length of his crack, leaving a long slick trail of saliva. Saliva was glistening and dripping from Jen's pink asshole as Heather stood up and took her own big, hard cock in her hand.

Jen purred. Knowing what was coming, he began to bend forward. His long, graceful body stretched forward at the waist till he could press his palms to the floor.

"Good girl," Heather said as she began to rub the tip of her beautiful cock down Jen's wet crack. She lowered her throbbing meat till it was even with Jen's dripping wet hole.

Jen bit his lip in expectation. He could still hear the sound of the man, rubbing his cock as he watched. Finally, Heather's bulging tip began to push forward into Jen's quivering rectum. Jen sighed deeply as his ass began to fill with the sensation of heat and pulsating. Tingles of raw pleasure, mixed with tingles of deeply implanted need that had been hypnotized into him, combined to fill him with immediate ecstasy.

Heather made adorable whimpers as she began to thrust her throbbing cock back and forth in Jen's soft asshole. Jen's body rocked back and forth, tits and erection jiggling as he felt the ridges and contours of Heather's perfect dick plunging inside him. Heather didn't hold anything back, she plowed him savagely, her fiery red hair swaying as the tiny muscles of her slinky frame worked.

Jen heard the sound of bare wet feet on the floor to his left and he turned his face to see Ting stepping out of the shower. The curvaceous little Asian looked stunning; mocha skin glistening with water droplets; dark wet hair shimmering; a small towel covering her from nipples to crotch, tucked in to the platform of her magnificent tits. Jen smiled at the lovely Asian doll. He didn't remember how long he had known Ting, but he felt like she had always been part of him. Ting smiled back, watching him fondly as his ass got hammered by the sexy, pale redhead.

Ting watched the model-perfect blonde he loved getting hammered by the waifish redhead with the big, gorgeous cock. Jen's body swayed back and forth with every thrust of Heather's hips, both their pairs of tits jiggling. Jen's small erection moved as well, slapping against her pelvis as she was hammered to and fro, blonde hair swaying and high, pretty voice whimpering.

On the bed in front of the pair, the man they were traveling with was stroking his fat, curved erection and also watching the pair with lust. Ting let his towel fall to the floor and leaned back against the sink. He grabbed a handful of one of his luscious artificial breasts and squeezed it. He grabbed his little erection between his finger than thumb and began to rub it.

The man rose from the bed, letting his thick meat swing in front of him like a battering ram as he walked towards the two trannies. His feet planted a few inches in front of Jen's hands and he bent forward, taking a fistful of Jen's luxurious blonde hair. He lifted Jen's slim torso up using the handle of her golden, shimmering hair. Her face turned up, eagerly accepting the sensation of being pulled up by her locks as her mouth fell open, level with the man's hot, throbbing cock.

Jen pressed her palms now against the man's thighs, bracing herself as the man rolled his hips forward and began to drive his fat meat into her soft, wet mouth. Jen's luscious lips closed around the man's thick shaft. He drove his cock deep into her throat, pressing his pelvis against her face, then he began to rollback, his cock now glistening with saliva. He continued to guide the little blonde by the hair as Heather guided her by the hips, pressing her slender young body back and forth between them.

Dexter began to really fuck Jen's mouth now, matching the intensity and power of Heather, who mercilessly pounded her tight little asshole. They both hammered the little blonde, fucking her harder and harder in both her ass and her throat as they both moaned with pleasure.

Ting moaned with pleasure too, his fingers tight along his slim erection, squeezing it as he pinched one of his pointed pink nipples. All around him were mirrors, showing his own sexy feminized body, impossibly slim in one spot, then incredibly vivacious the next, his skin all shimmering a light, creamy brown. Ting loved being surrounded by his own luscious reflection as he stroked his little dick and watched the gurl he loved get fucked on both ends by two big cocks.

Dexter had one hand tight in Jen's blonde curls. He reached across Jen's body to Heather, gripping one of Heather's firm tits and squeezing it, feeling the delicious resistance of the silicone beneath his palm. Heather smiled at him, her eyes full of lust as she pumped away at Jen's taught pink asshole, and Dexter pumped away at her little, wet mouth.

Ting squeezed his little dick between his fingertip and thumb, jerking it up and down as he watched the slender body of the model-perfect blonde get bounced between the cock of a hot young tranny and the cock of a hairy, middle-aged man. He could imagine the ecstasy Jen was feeling; fat contours of dick throbbing in the soft flesh of her openings, plunging deep inside, filling her with powerful vibrations and a deep sense of purpose. Ting knew Jen craved being the center of attention even more than he did, so he continued to let her have it, watching from a distance as his little, hairless balls began to tingle and his pink erection began to twitch.

Drool ran down the bottom of Jen's Botox filled lip, running in a long shimmering line that waved beneath her like her unused sissy erection as she was fucked back and forth between two big cocks. All Jen's doll training was paying off, as she easily took the brutal pounding of both those hot, hard slabs of meat. Ting could see the cocks stretching her open as they impaled the sultry blonde over and over. Jen's luscious lips and tender asshole clinging to the thick contours of both rods as they pushed back and forth with growing speed. The room was full of sounds, the wet slurping of Jen's eager mouth, the slapping of Heather's pale flesh against Jen's perfectly tanned ass, the man grunting, Heather's feminine voice purring with pleasure as she rammed her cock forward and back.

Ting's whole body was shuddering. He tightened his grip on his soft, round breast as the intensity became too much to bear. His feet flex flexed, his painted toenails spreading on the linoleum floor as his cock began to erupt up into his face and across his gorgeous tits. Ting gasped as hot sprays of his own semen shot across his gorgeous Asian face in long white strings, splattering across his cheeks and splashing into his open mouth.

Jen was slipping over the edge too, her body shaking as it continued to be rammed back and forth, her own little prick began sputtering out wads of cream onto the floor beneath her. The sperm jetted from her untouched dick as Jen experienced the type of true orgasm a sissy could only get from deep anal penetration. The Jets of warm spunk squirted out with every thrust of Heather's hips, Jen's mouth too stuffed full of cock for her to whimper or moan. Ting looked at Jen's glistening semen on the floor as the gorgeous blonde continued to be hammered at both ends. The thick wads of sperm glazed the dirty motel floor and Ting couldn't resist its creamy allure. He rushed forward and dropped to his hands and knees. Sliding under Jen, Ting began to lap up the filthy cream.

Heather shuddered and a moment later, she too was climaxing. Heather fired her first few spurt of jizz into Jen's asshole, but then she jerked herself free and began to spray steaming wads of spunk across Jen's gorgeous, slender back. The thick cream splattered against Jen's supple skin, covering it in a shimmering glaze. As soon as Heather finished emptying her balls, she leaned forward and began to lick the fresh sperm off Jen's tantalizing flesh.

Dexter watched the redhead, tits pressed against the small of Jen's back, lapping up her own sperm with darting flicks of her little pink tongue and he groaned, overcome by intensity. He drove his cock deep down Jen's throat and began to erupt into her esophagus. Jen didn't gag or cough. The skilled little cocksucker didn't react in any way other than to gulp down each thick, salty wad that shot from the cock buried down her throat.

Jen felt the comforting heat of Dexter's cock bulging in his throat as Heather's tongue lapped at the hot cream she'd splattered across his back. Jen heard Dexter moan and felt him shudder as his dick twitched in Jen's narrow throat, spurting jets of hot cum. Dexter's hands were twisted in his luscious blonde curls, the man probably not even realizing how hard he was yanking on Jen's scalp, but Jen didn't mind. He liked the thrill of the pain as he continued gulping enthusiastically, his esophagus tight with suction as he drained the man's balls into his tiny, surgically restricted stomach.

Dexter sighed as the pulled his softening dick from between Jen's luscious lips. Ting sat up from the floor as Jen sat back on his heels. Ting brought her cum glistening lips to Jen's and they began to kiss passionately. Heather joined them, bringing her own glazed lips to the mix and joining them in a wet, salty three-way kiss. They kissed for a while then they held hands and joined Dexter on the motel bed.

They all cuddled and fell asleep, dozing comfortably in each other's arms until they woke up in the middle of the night, their dicks all hard and their bodies hungry more filthy fucking.

Shemale Interrogation Techniques

Dexter walked out of the motel room, leaving the three gorgeous trannies sleeping on his bed. He couldn't believe it had only been a few days since he'd picked them up. They had been travelling along the highway, stopping at cheap motels and fucking day and night. He had never even seen such beautiful creatures as these young girls before, and he'd never in his life had this much sex. Part of him knew it couldn't last. They were too hot for him, and it was only a matter of time till he screwed it up. But he wasn't going to worry about that. He was going to enjoy every minute of the filthy ride.

He walked down the dark sidewalk to a snack machine that sat beside the drained pool. He bought a candy-bar, then bought three more to offer the girls. He knew he would end up just eating them all himself. That was okay. The skinny little transgender hitchhikers didn't seem interested in solid food, but he was starving.

He walked back towards the room, opening a Snickers and munching on it when another beautiful woman caught his eye. It seemed an odd coincidence to see another girl so breathtaking in this sleazy motel in the middle of nowhere.

The woman he saw was a tiny, slim brunette. She was standing next to two very large men in black t-shirts. The two men looked like bouncers or bodyguards as they stood ominously over the stunning, petite girl. She stopped a passing trucker and drew his attention to a series of three pictures. Dexter could hear the woman's sensuous voice drifting from across the parking lot as she purred, "Have you seen any of these girls?"

Dexter didn't know what his gorgeous transgender dolls were hiding from, but he knew they were on the run. He dropped his candy and hurried back to the room. He started throwing the girls their clothes. "Someone's here," he told them. "Someone's out there looking for you."

The girls began to panic and rushed out of the bed, naked except for slinky lace panties. "What do we do?" Ting asked him, as if he had the slightest clue what was really happening here.

"Sneak out the back window," he told them. "I'll go out the front and get the van. I'll pull around the back and meet you."

The girls rushed into the bathroom, throwing on their clothes as they waited their turn to shimmy out the bathroom window.

Dexter watched them all escape, then he waited a minute to regain his calm. He looked in the mirror to verify he looked perfectly natural, then he walked to the door and prepared to step outside. He pulled open the door and was suddenly standing in front of the small, beautiful brunette. In heels she stood just a few inches over five foot, with dark supple skin and lustrous dark hair. She wore a tight black dress that squeezed her small breasts and hugged her petite frame. She looked cute and almost girlish, but she looked at him with dark, commanding eyes.

"Where are they?" she demanded.

"Who?"

The two guards pushed into the room and the lovely brunette strolled in behind them as if she were a conquering general. “Don’t make me repeat myself,” she said. “It bores me.”

Dexter swallowed. The two guards were young and massive and powerful, looming on either side of the woman, so why was it her he was terrified of?

“I don’t know. They left a long time ago,” he said.

She stepped forward, her movement slow and sensuous. She moved into his personal space, her presence hot and electric. He had the strange, tingling feeling that she was about to kiss him as her body moved within an inch of his, but instead she slapped him hard across the face. He winced and grabbed his cheek. She stared at him a tiny crooked smile on her beautiful face.

“You filthy, weak little thing. You can’t lie to my mistress. I won’t allow it.” She slapped him hard across the face again, then actually giggled when it brought tears to his eyes.

“I’m sorry, Sweetie,” she said mockingly. “Did I hurt you?” She stepped even closer, her soft, tight little body pressing against him as she reached down and grabbed his crotch. She squeezed his balls through his slacks making him whimper. She began twisting them painfully as she smiled up into his face. “Are you sensitive?” she asked. She squeezed harder, twisting more. “Answer my question please.”

Dexter grit his teeth in pain, even as he felt a strange burst of tingling excitement rushing to his cock. He took a deep breath, shocked and ashamed that his dick was beginning to swell. But he wasn’t the only one getting hard, Dexter realized with horror. He could feel it pressing against his thigh and looked down in disbelief. He saw the unmistakable imprint of a massive erection bulging against the thin fabric of the Brunette’s skin-tight dress.

Dexter couldn't speak as he stared at the big bulge in the beautiful girl's dress. She rose up on her toes as she twisted his balls even more. "Please," he whimpered, but he couldn't hide how hard she was making him.

She stared up at him. "Begging isn't going to help you," she said. "But do please continue. I do enjoy the sound of it."

"Miss," he started to say.

"Call me Bridgett, Worm," she said.

"Bridgett," he grunted, wincing with pain. "I picked up three hitch-hikers a few days ago. I dropped them off several towns back two days past and that's the last I saw of them."

Bridgett smiled. "You're lying to me. I'm glad. I wanted to punish you the minute I saw your gross, hairy body and sloppy clothes. I wanted a reason to hurt you since the first moment I heard your whining voice." She suddenly released her iron grip on his balls and he gasped with relief. She turned around, giving him a chance to stare at her petite frame as she stepped towards the door. "Strip and face the other wall," she commanded.

He stood there trembling, staring at the dark, striking tranny with the commanding presence. He didn't move from his spot.

She reached around the door and grabbed a small bag she had left there. She turned back to him and looked at him with her dark, shimmering eyes. "Strip or I'll have you stripped," she said simply.

With shaking hands, Dexter began to strip out of his clothes, slowly revealing his pale, hairy, middle-aged body.

Bridgett looked at it, laughing at him as he stripped. He was almost relieved when he turned towards the wall, because he didn't have to see her dark, mockery filled eyes.

"Filthy, filthy man," Bridgett said. "What are we going to do with you? A filthy, disobedient liar. What good could you possibly serve?"

She pulled a three-pronged whip from her bag and unfurled the long leather thongs letting them stretch across the floor as she held it below the slender curve of her hip.

"I'm not lying," he whimpered.

"Another lie," she stated in her cool, sensual voice. She lifted her arm and swung the whip threw the air, whistling it down on his ass.

Dexter howled as the sharp pain bit into him, making his teeth grit. It was almost like being burned, a quick intense pain followed by the stinging relief of its passing. His dick was harder than ever.

"You are a worthless, pointless man. You are a piece of garbage who has no value."

"I have value," he whimpered.

"Another lie," Bridgett said, slashing him across his pale, hairy thighs.

Dexter's cock throbbed with thrilling intensity as his thighs screamed with pain. Part of him wished he could just agree with the beautiful shemale. Part of him wished he didn't feel the need to defend his value so desperately. Hadn't his whole life been unraveling for a long time. If it wasn't for the hitchhikers, he would say he had always been the world's biggest loser. Was it really so bad just to give in?

Again the belt cut across his ass. Again he cried out in shocking pain, but his dick was dribbling precum, the sound of Bridgett's voice running up his spine as she purred, "You are worthless. You are my worthless little toy. The sooner you admit that to yourself the sooner I can find something useful for you to do."

Dexter thought of the erection throbbing in the beautiful shemale's dress. He wanted to be useful to that petite little vixen. He wanted to service that gorgeous beauty in any way he could. "I'm worthless," he said. "I'm a worthless little toy. I'm a pathetic little bitch."

He flinched, expecting the whip to slash across him once more but it didn't.

"Turn around," Bridgett purred. "And get on your knees where you belong."

Dexter turned around, naked and humiliated, his ass burning and his cock throbbing. He dropped to his knees. The stunning brunette smiled down at him as she took the hem of her dress in her fingertips and began to wiggle it up her dark legs, hiking her dress up the slender curve of her hips past her black lace panties. She pulled her panties aside, freeing her massive hardon. She moved her small, spinner frame closer, pushing her big dick towards his lips.

"Show me you have some value, little bitch," she said.

Dexter looked from the trannies big, pink cock to her the nipples of her small breasts pressing against the fabric of her skin-tight dress. He looked up at her beautiful, angry face and waves of dark hair. He looked back at her long, straight cock, then he glanced at the two bodyguards. They stared blankly as if it all meant nothing to them one way or the other. They were only there to enforce the beautiful tranny's will, but

Bridgett's will did not need enforcing. Dexter's mouth was salivating with forbidden need.

His own cock was throbbing in his lap as he leaned forward and opened his mouth, breathing in the fresh, floral scent of Bridgett's tight, little hormone altered body. Bridgett pushed her hips forward, pressing the tip of her bulging prick into Dexter's open mouth. Dexter felt a sudden shock as the gravity of the moment sunk in. It was dick he was tasting, his lips pressing to the hot crown as the tip rested on his tongue. He tasted salt and felt heat as the tip moved forward slowly, pressing across the spongy surface of his palette. Bridgett's hands caressed his thin hair almost affectionately for a moment, then they tightened, pulling his strands taught in her grip.

Dexter stared up at the beautiful shemale and she smiled wickedly as she suddenly plunged her cock forward, driving it into his virgin throat. Her narrow frame, with luscious skin and gently curving, delicate hips looked delicious and thrilling as her cock rammed suddenly down his esophagus. Dexter gagged as his throat was invaded with bulging meat.

Bridgett smiled as she watched him struggle, his eyes watering and his face turning red as she drew her hips back and drove her cock forward again.

Dexter struggled to relax as he gagged on hard, hot prick. He reached forward and touched the slender tranny's thin brown legs, feeling the silky-smooth flesh of her thighs with his sweaty palms.

Neither Dexter's struggle nor his hands slowed Bridgett as she rocked her hips back and forth, driving her cock in and out of his throat. "Get that cock nice and wet," Bridgett said as she fucked his mouth. "The more slippery you make it, the easier it will go in, and the less it will hurt when I ram your tight, virgin asshole."

Dexter's body trembled with fear and anticipation. He willed more saliva to flood his mouth, coating the tranny's thick pole in glimmering drool as it pumped back and forth in his throat.

"Good little bitch," Bridgett said softly. She held his skull in place as she pulled her dong from between his lips. It was coated in saliva, but she softly commanded, "Spit on the tip."

Dexter, struggling to catch his breath, pressed his lips to the bulging pink head and spit a glob of spittle onto it. The thick puddle of drool shined on the spongy tip, dribbling down it in a long, shiny strand.

"Turn around, Worm," Bridgett said.

Dexter was shaking as he obeyed.

"Head down, ass up," Bridgett ordered. "Spread those ass-cheeks nice and wide for me."

The bodyguards watched indifferently as Dexter pressed his cheek against the dirty linoleum floor. He hesitated there, unable to surrender the last shred of his manhood. "I'm not sure I want this," he said.

"No one cares what you want," Bridgett reminded him. "Spread."

Dexter swallowed hard and reached behind himself, pulling himself open.

Bridgett's purring, feminine voice rolled up his spine. "A loser like you should be grateful just to be in the same room with me." She knelt behind him and pressed her swollen pink cockhead to his trembling brown hole.

He could feel the tremendous heat and throbbing of blood-filled flesh against his sensitive skin. His body responded with tingling as he ached with hunger. He didn't want this, he realized, he needed it.

He took a deep breath and closed his eyes. The petite shemale moaned as she began to penetrate him. The sharp pain of his asshole stretching around the tranny's big, hard cock made him wince and whimper. "Oh fuck," he cried.

Bridgett continued to impale him, her throbbing meat pushing into his soft, tender flesh. The pain of her expanding and reshaping his bowels made him bite his tongue to keep from screaming out, but he was also overwhelmed with a powerful shudder as his entire consciousness became overloaded by the warm presence of another human being inside him.

"Good Bitch," Bridgett said, pushing her prick deeper inside him. He felt her small hands grip his hips with surprising strength as she grinded herself all the way inside him, pulsating with heat and electricity.

Dexter's rectum burned and ached. His skin tingled where the tranny's soft flesh made contact with him, her soft hips against his ass-cheeks, her slender thighs pressing against him. He was drooling onto the floor, oblivious of everything but the throbbing cock of the beautiful shemale inside him. His dick was still rock-hard.

She grinded her soft flesh against him, pushing her bulging cockhead deep through the depths of his anus. He whimpered as she began to withdraw from him, making him shiver with suction as the vacuum of his tight asshole was worked by her big dick. She moved backwards several inches then plunged forward once more, her sexy voice releasing a pleasured whimper as she impaled him.

She pulled back again, this time a little farther, then rocked forward a little harder. Dexter planted his palms onto the floor to keep from being flattened down as she began to repeat this movement, slamming into him harder with every thrust. He groaned with aching pain as he was repeatedly hollowed out and filled again with the tranny's thick, pulsating rod. One moment he felt the painful presence of her rock-hard erection battering into him, and the next he felt the aching relief of her pulling back, leaving his bowels a freshly plowed void.

In spite of the burning agony of the increasingly savage fucking, Dexter began to shiver with strange jolts of intense pleasure. He could feel it across the surface of his skin, in the vibrating core of his prostate, and all along the length of his own pulsating cock.

"Where are they?" Bridgett demanded.

"I'll tell you anything you want," he cried. "Just don't stop. Please don't stop."

She continued to ram him, her pole burrowing through the ring of his sphincter and plunging into the soft depths of his colon. He had lost all sense of time and place, his body was being rocked back and forth with each thrust, his face dragging across the dirty motel floor. A powerful heat and intense vibration was building inside him. The vibrations and heat pulsated from his bowels and his prostate and began to throb through his balls into the shaft of his dick. He was harder than he'd ever been before as his rod began to twitch beneath him, the sheath of his asshole clinging to and stretching around the bulging flesh of the stunning tranny's cock.

He whimpered as the sensation grew more and more intense with every rough, indifferent thrust of the shemale's thin, feminine frame. Suddenly the feeling exploded inside him.

Every inch of his flesh tingled with pinpricks of ecstasy as his balls pulled up and his dick quaked and jerked beneath him, beginning to shoot sperm in hot jets across his own tummy and chest.

The orgasm didn't stop at his dick, it continued to ripple through him long after the last thick splatter of cum shot from his balls. He moaned and cried, the pleasure of continuous climax overtaking the intense pain that still racked through his anal cavity. He continued to rock back and forth in a blissful state of oblivion as the shemale continued to hammer his ass with her rock-hard prick.

Finally, Bridgett whimpered deliciously. Dexter could feel her cock swell even more as she plunged deep inside his colon and began to erupt creamy semen into his quivering void. He could feel the hot, filthy jizz splattering against the raw, pummeled flesh of his hole and it sent him spinning into another intense orgasm.

Once more Dexter's dick began to twitch, as if shooting more cream, but his balls were dry, his dick pulsating with ecstasy as his whole body reverberated with blissful vibration. Finally, the feeling passed and Dexter collapsed forward, limp and spent.

Bridgett wiped her softening cock clean with Dexter's t shirt, then tossed the shirt aside as she stood once more. She grabbed the edge of her sexy lace panties and tucked herself back into them, then wiggled her hips as she pulled the hem of her dress back down. "Where are they?" she asked, her soft dick now just a subtle but shocking bulge in her skin-tight dress.

"They climbed out the window," Dexter said in a drained, blissful daze. "Right before you got here."

Bridgett looked at one of her guards. "Come with me," she ordered. She looked at the other and said, "Bring this one to the car." She poked Dexter with the toe of one of her lovely black heels. "He's amusing."

Biker Bar Bunnies

In the final hours of the night, three beautiful women ran half-naked into a bar. They looked like beautiful women anyway: Their hair soft and lustrous, bodies curved and delicious, skin supple and glowing. They had tiny waists and curving hips. Their faces were permanently tattooed with makeup, but more was added, giving them a sleazy, wanton look. They wore bra's and shorts, blouses open and flapping in the air behind them.

When they stepped through the door, everyone stopped and looked at them. They were too impossibly beautiful to be in the same room together. The blonde had the grace and body of a lingerie model, the redhead the slinky frame and commanding presence of a movie-star. The Asian had lush, artificial curves that could have only been built for porn. They stood in the doorway, looking at the crowd of bikers staring back at them.

The men in the bar wore weather worn leather and had weather worn faces. They had rough tattoos and strong builds. Most of them had dangerous eyes.

Jen felt all the stares of those mean-looking men and felt a flutter in his stomach. His dick tingled in his panties as he began to smile beamingly. Heather snatched him by the wrist and dragged him and Ting away from the doorway and to the darkest corner of the bar. Most of the men just stared, but three of the most dangerous looking men in the bar stood up and began to follow them. The three men all had leather vests decorated with the same flaming skull, the word "Violators" printed in gothic letters above it.

The youngest of the men was in his twenties, lean and long like a basketball player. His name was on his vest in blood red letters, "Spike." He would have looked clean cut if it weren't for the sprawling tattoos covering every inch of his body, including most of his face. The oldest was probably in his fifties, built wide and tall like a mountain man, his skin rough from weather and scars but his body looking solid as a brick wall, his name read "Wild Man." The shortest one was in his thirties, he looked like a weight lifter, his hair shaved and his mouth twisted into a snarl. His name read "Buzz."

Jen stood looking at the three men, arching his slim back to show off his artificial tits and smiling beautifully. He had already forgotten what they were running from, but he was glad they had run here. He raised his hand and gave the men a dainty little wave.

Ting and Heather stood close at either side of Jen, their gorgeous bodies also being salivated over by the savage looking bikers.

The oldest one spoke, his big frame commanding the entire space. "Hello ladies," Wild Man said. "What brings you out on a night like this?"

Heather met his eyes and spoke in her thrilling, sensuous voice. "We're running from some bad people."

Buzz laughed. "Bad people?" he said, his massive sculpted arms flexing. "Shit girl. There aint nobody as bad as us."

The young one spoke now. Spike said, "Nobody will hurt you if were around. But we lose interest easy. Most girls have to show us their tits just to get our attention." He turned to Buzz, laughing at his own joke, then his eyes went wide when he looked back and saw Jen had already pulled off his bra.

Jen stood smiling, wearing nothing but tight denim shorts and an open blouse, his big, silicone tits jetting out from a slim torso.

Spike smiled now. "Shit," he said. "You are a little freak, aren't you?" He looked at Ting and said, "What about you?"

Ting slipped off her open jacket and let it fall to the floor, then she undid her bra and released her magnificent brown breasts.

"Hell yeah," the young biker said. "This is going to be fun." He was still staring at Ting. "Now take off those shorts."

Ting swallowed and looked to Heather, who shook her head slightly, her eyes full of warning. Ting looked back at the young biker, but it just wasn't in her to disobey the command of a real man. She undid her tiny shorts and shimmied her body out of them. She wasn't wearing panties and her tiny, limp penis hung like a delicate worm above her hairless balls.

Spike stared at the little Asian tranny, taking in her luscious tits, tiny waist, curving hips, supple feminine skin. He took it all in then he looked at her little dick and tiny hairless balls. "What the hell are you?" he asked.

"Whatever you want us to be," was Ting's soft, sensual reply.

There was a moment when no one spoke. Jen could feel the tension in the air and it made his nipples hard and his knees weak. His ass was suddenly aching to be filled.

"Fuck it," Wild Man said, stepping up to the circle of shemales. "She looks pretty good to me." He stepped up in front of Ting and opened his jeans. He pulled them down enough to reveal his big, limp cock. He let it dangle as he made eye contact with the slim Asian, then nodded down.

Ting instantly dropped to her knees.

The bikers on the other side of the bar had been keeping their distance from the "Violators." It was clear to Jen that these three men where the important ones. They were very important men.

Jen felt uncomfortable standing so close to a group of very important men without any of their throbbing dicks in his mouth, so he moved beside the beautiful Asian, stripping off his shorts as he dropped to his knees. As Ting wrapped her lips around the soft head of the man's limp penis, Jen wiggled closer and began to kiss his balls. The man moaned, his dick beginning to swell in Ting's mouth. Ting looked up at the man with her dark, exotic eyes, her cheeks sucking in as she sucked his hardening cock with all her might. Jen began to flick the man's balls with his little pink tongue, moving from one to the other, breathing in the manly smells of sweat, leather and gasoline.

Buzz moved forward with purpose, but Spike stood watching with indecision. Spike's face was full of horror in spite of the erection that was pressing against his jeans. Buzz stepped up to Heather, looking the long, slinky redhead up and down. "You a little tranny freak too?"

Heather nodded, her eyes fixed on the man, her incredibly long legs seeming to bow out slightly in invitation.

"Show me," Buzz said.

Heather stripped out of her clothes, revealing her supple, freckled skin. She looked like miles of young, hormone softened paradise. She left her panties on, but she couldn't hide the big, semi erect cock she had tucked into it.

Buzz laughed, but he was hard in his jeans. He pointed a finger and poked Heather through her panties with a quick painful jab. "You ever fuck with that thing?" he asked.

Heather nodded again as her dick swelled, excited to be touched, even with a brief painful finger-jab. Her perfectly formed pink dick pushed out of her little silk thong, pointing up at her beautiful, natural looking tits.

Buzz looked from Heather to Ting. "Go fuck your little friend," he said.

Ting's lips moved up and down Wild Man's now rock-hard prick, cradling his hot meat as she slurped and sucked loudly. Jen continued to tease the man's balls with his little pink tongue, breathing in the powerful scent of manhood. Ting let the biker's big dick slip from her mouth and turned her face to Jen. Jen smiled up at the tantalizing Asian and they began to kiss passionately, their wet tongues squishing in and out of each other's drooling mouths. They kissed for a minute, then began licking up and down Wild Man's cock, their tongues lapping at his thick, throbbing meat as they brushed against each other.

Jen was in paradise, sharing a dick and a kiss with the gurl he loved. He lapped up the strings of saliva that Ting drooled on the hot meat. He flicked his tongue across Ting's lips and the man's dick, breathing in the scent of testosterone, sweat, and Ting's minty, pink mouth. Ting moved to the man's tip once more and spread her luscious lips to swallow the rough, older biker's big throbbing cock. Her lips cradled his bulging meat like glistening red pillows as she took the man in and out of her throat.

Heather moved up and dropped to her knees behind Ting. Heather took hold of Ting's curving hips and pulled them back, making her soft, pink asshole available.

Ting purred with delicious anticipation, her back arching and her little prick erect. Jen was hard too, his own sissy clit throbbing between his slim feminine thighs as he continued to lap at Wild Man's dick, following Ting's lips up and down the shaft. The bulging pink tip of Heather's gorgeous dick began to press into Ting's tight hole. Ting released a muffled moan against the flesh of Wild Man's cock as Heather's cock began to impale her.

Ting's little prick dribbled precum, her mouth stuffed with cock and her ass being split open with hard meat.

Heather whimpered with pleasure as she penetrated the gorgeous Asian's tight asshole. The sound of Heather's voice, high and feminine, squeaking with every thrust as she plunged her meat into Ting, was thrilling and Jen couldn't resist stroking his own little prick as he continued to lap at Wild Man's dick and balls.

Buzz just watched, seeing Heather's firm tits jiggle slightly as she fucked the Asian, the Asian's big tits swaying beneath her as she bounced back and forth between two cocks. The man was hard in his jeans, watching the filthy scene till he couldn't take it anymore. He dropped his jeans to his ankles and stepped behind Heather, his fat, monstrous dick leading the way. He used a rough, calloused hand to push on the back of Heather's slim neck, pressing her face down on Ting's slender brown back.

Heather's pale, freckled skin contrasted Ting's deep mocha flesh, red hair wild and streaming down Ting's sides, dick still buried in Ting's asshole. Buzz spread Heather's small ass-cheeks and spit on her crack, then he pressed forward. Heather moaned as the man pushed his swollen tip to her tender asshole, then whimpered as he began to enter her. Jen stroked his own needy little dick, his body tingling with hunger as he continued to worship Wild Man's old balls and rock-hard prick.

From a few feet away, the youngest one just watched. Spike had a horrified look on his young face, but his hardon still throbbed unmistakably in his jeans. Buzz began fucking Heather, his dick slamming deep inside the gorgeous redhead. With each thrust, Buzz pushed Heather forward, causing her dick to thrust deep into Ting. The force of the thrust continued, driving Ting's lips down Wild Man's shaft. Jen could feel the final vibrations of the thrust as they tingled across the man's balls to Jen's little pink mouth.

The force then reversed itself, Wild Man slamming Ting's mouth, sending her whole-body rocking back against Heather, Heather back against buzz, everybody moaning with pleasure or gagging on cock.

Jen jerked his cock, slurping up the drool at that trickled from Ting's mouth as Ting was fucked back and forth, her mouth sliding up and down Wild Man's pole.

Heather's wet mouth moaned against the flesh of Ting's supple back, both of their tender asshole's split open by fat, throbbing dick.

The last biker's eyes were locked on Jen, his expression had started to change from horror to lust as he eyed Jen's flawless curving frame. Jen eyed the young man, begging with deep blue eyes for him to come join the party, while continuing to lap obediently at Wild Man's big, hairy balls. Spike finally gave in, beginning to strip as he walked forward.

Jen watched with an excited shudder as the Spike's lean, tattoo-covered body became revealed, his long prick was hard and pointing forward, vein-crossed and rippled with contours. Jen let his lips slip from Wild Man's balls as the youngest biker grabbed Jen's slim ankles and pulled him closer. With a jerk of the hands, Spike flipped Jen onto his back on the floor. Jen did not resist as the young man splayed his long, slender legs apart and knelt between them. Jen still had his little hardon in his hand, jerking it frantically as Spike took his own, fat prick and pressed it to Jen's opening.

Jen shuddered with excitement, looking from Spike's lean, chiseled body to Ting's curved feminine frame, to Heather's tall wispy body, fucking Ting's ass as her own ass was plowed by a muscle-bound biker. Ting gargled and drooled as she was fucked back and forth on the old, mountain man's huge throbbing dick.

Spike took hold of Jen's tiny waist and lusciously curved hips, then he smashed his body forward, ripping into Jen's ass savagely. Jen cried out as the big cock violated his dry asshole, but his dick jumped, spilling out a huge load of precum that dribbled down his shaft and coated his hand. The precum ran down his balls and his crack, dripping onto the young biker's shaft. The biker moaned as he began to hump Jen's tight asshole. Jen moaned as he felt the long meat punching deep inside his sissy womb. The biker's fingers held his waist tightly, gripping his soft flesh with savage indifference as he pounded Jen's quivering hole.

Jen's high-pitched whimpers mirrored Heather's feminine cries as they both had their assholes reamed. Ting gargled and groaned on cock as her own sissy-cunt was fucked. All three shemale voices filled the room, moving in time to the dicks that pounded them.

Jen pressed his smooth heels to the back of Spike's thighs, staring up at the powerful young man. The man grimaced down at Jen's beautiful face. He grabbed one of Jen's lush artificial breasts, squeezing it mercilessly with an iron grip as his cock hammered the sissy's slender hole. Jen clutched his own little prick, two fingers tight around it as if strangling it as they moved up and down in time to the dick that pounded his rectum.

Jen could hear the slapping of flesh, Buzz on Heather, Heather on Ting, Spike on his own lush sissy ass. He could hear the slurping of cock as his beloved Ting slobbered along the length of Wild Man's dick. Jen arched his back and worked his hips, grinding his body against Spike as the young biker plunged his bulging cockhead through Jen's soft, pink insides.

The sounds and smells and sensations of all that fucking, sucking and stroking made Jen's head spin. The room seemed to vibrate with intensity. He whimpered, overwhelmed with the sensation that he was a piece of the machinery in a huge, out of control fucking machine. "Yes," Jen whimpered. "Yes. Fuck my sissy-cunt. Use me like trash. I love it when you fuck me hard."

Spike grunted as he pummeled Jen's asshole, Jen's intestines bulging with cock.

Jen wasn't the only one who could feel it. He looked at Ting, her slim erection bouncing against her tummy as she was hammered at both ends. Ting's body was trembling in ecstasy, her dick beginning to spurt, splattering semen against her own tummy and tits, then dripping down onto the floor.

Heather cried out as she began to shoot her own load in the Asian trannies ass, filling the slender brown girl with hot white cum. Buzz pulled his cock from Heather's ass, shooting his cream in massive strings across Heather's pale flesh, splattering her slim thighs, cute ass and narrow back, as Heather continued to writhe in ecstasy against Ting's back.

Wild man groaned as he began to unload his balls into Ting's throat. Ting's throat worked visibly as she gulped down every thick, salty wad of sperm.

"Fuck!" Jen whimpered as his feminized body writhed at the end of Spike's big, throbbing cock. "Fuck!" The orgasm exploded inside him and outside him, his balls tightening as his sphincter locked down, his dick firing squirts of hot jizz across his tummy and tits as his prostate exploded in blissful vibration.

Spike pulled his fat cock from Jen's hole and added his own thick loads to the squirts of cum that Jen continued to shoot on his own hormone softened skin. Jen let go of his dick and began to rub the cream into his flesh as it continued to splatter down on him. He whimpered as he writhed, pulsating and sputtering out his own sperm while showering in Spike's hot spunk. Jen rubbed all that delicious semen into his flesh as he writhed in orgasm beneath the powerful young biker.

When Spike finished raining sperm on the gorgeous blonde tranny, he stood up and turned away. Everyone began to gather up their clothes. Jen felt a sinking sense of loss in his core, as if the great fuck-machine he was connected to had suddenly been shut off. Now that the passion had passed and he was panting and spent, it felt awkward to have to still exist. He longed to be gathered up and put back in his beautiful box, so he could rest until someone else wanted to play with his hot, feminized body.

Jen looked to the side and that's when he noticed her.

He had begun to believe the woman was imaginary, a goddess of legend and dream. But there she was, beautiful and graceful and radiant with Power. The woman's dark, petite assistant stood behind her, as the six-foot goddess sat elegantly waiting at a nearby table.

Tanya Payne smiled at Jen as he gathered himself up from the floor. She raised a graceful hand and waved for Jen to approach. Jen smiled blankly and began to walk towards the mesmerizing light of the gorgeous Mistress.

Ting and Heather grabbed her arms. "Wait," Heather said. "That's Tanya. That's who were trying to escape from."

Jen laughed. "Why?" She slithered from the girl's grasp and approached the beautiful Tanya Payne.

Jen felt like he was floating as he approached the table. Time seemed to skip ahead as he listened to the luscious voice and gazed into the deep eyes and voluptuous chest.

"My pet," Tanya purred. "My perfect little pet. How I've missed you. How my men have missed you. I think it's time to come home. Don't you?"

Jen whispered, "They say I should want to be free. They say I should escape you."

Tanya laughed. "That's because they don't know what they are. That's because they don't know where they belong. But you know, don't you Sweetie?"

Jen nodded, licking his Botox filled lips. "How did you find us?"

"You belong to me," Tanya purred. "I can feel your every thought and movement before you even make it. I would never have to do something like implant a crude GPS tracker inside your fake tits, that would be completely unnecessary. I own your deepest, most secret dreams. Come with me, doll. Get your friends and come home."

Jen listened to Tanya's mesmerizing voice as she painted the details of a deliciously sensual future where Jen would always be beautiful, and always be lusted after.

"I want that," Jen purred. "I want to come home with you."

"Good girl," Tanya purred. "Go tell your friends."

Jen got up and strolled back to his friends. They were dressed now and looking at him strangely. He had the impression that more time had passed then he realized.

Jen smiled, his eyes distant and blank. "She says she'll take us back. She forgives us."

Heather shook her head. "We escaped from her. We were her prisoners. Of course, she'll take us back. We're slaves to her."

Jen visibly shuddered at the word Slaves. "Fuck. I miss it so much," he said.

"Don't you see what happened," Heather said. "She just hypnotized you. You're under her power again."

Jen smiled a sparkling smile, the expression on his beautiful face full of blissful emptiness. "Yes," he purred.

Heather sighed. "You can do whatever you want, Sweetie. But I'm not going back. The Bikers said we can go with them. They won't let her take us against our will. You don't have to be afraid. We have protection."

Jen smiled. "I can't live without Tanya Payne. I can't live without her controlling my thoughts and using my body. I'm so tired of not knowing what to do or what to say or what to think. I miss having someone to tell me." He turned to Ting. "Don't be mad at me. I love you."

Ting took the model-perfect blonde's hand. "I love you too," she said. "And where you go, I go. If you need to go back, then I need to go back with you."

"Okay," Heather said. "But I'm not going back. I'm staying with The Violators. Tanya Payne can chase me all she wants. I'm not going."

"I guess this is goodbye then," Ting said.

"Yes," Heather said. "I'm going to miss you two stupid, sexy bitches."

"We'll miss you too," Jen purred.

The three gorgeous trannies were crying. They all embraced each other and mashed their lips together in a sloppy-wet three-way kiss goodbye.

Biker Gurl Gang Initiation

Heather shuddered with pleasure as he looked at his sexy new sissy uniform, laid out on the table. The skin-tight leather skirt and a slinky leather vest glistened in the light. The vest had an emblem on the back, the emblem of the flaming skull with the words, "Violator's Bitch" written beneath it. As sexy as those where, Heather's hands went straight to the little leather dog collar.

Heather had been with the gang for weeks now. He hadn't seen any sign of Tanya coming after him, but he knew it was only a matter of time. Right now, these rough and savage men where his only protection, but that was okay, because he liked the price of securing their favor. He was their bitch and their fuck-meat, but he still felt freer then he could ever remember. He loved the feeling of the wind in his silky red hair as it streamed behind him on the back of one of the guys bikes. He could usually choose who he rode with in the day, and he had some say in who he got fucked by in the night. Some nights the guys would pick up a sleazy young hitchhiker or wanna-be model headed for the nearest big city. The guys loved watching their own pet tranny seduce and fuck the young girls, and Heather loved being the center of attention as the men drank and catcalled and watched him fuck.

Heather's hand hovered over the dog-collar for a while, then he finally picked it up from the grimy folding table. His whole body tingled with a sense of belonging when he saw the words, sissy pet, engraved in the leather. He didn't hesitate to toss his flaming red waves aside and strap the collar to his long, elegant neck. He could feel the eyes of the whole gang on his slinky feminine curves, as he stood alone in the center of the old warehouse turned clubhouse, wearing nothing but a pair of little pink panties.

Wild Man stepped out of the crowd and approached. He had a distant, formal air as he handed Heather the final piece of his uniform. A black, steel chastity cage with a big, pink gothic V printed on the tip. Heather took the cock-locking device like it was a sacred prize and snapped it over his big, limp dick. Wild man took a padlock and locked the device closed. Heather shuddered with the sense of finality of the act. But he could see there was a key for it, dangling from the biker's belt. Perhaps they would still unlock him for fun, perhaps watching as he fucked other girls, or other guys, Heather didn't care. He could feel Tanya Payne's conditioning still coursing through him, making him want to fuck or get fucked by anyone. But mostly he just wanted to be useful. He wanted to be sexy and useful and as much fun as humanly possible.

Heather bowed to the massive, older man, loving his rough, hairy face. "Thank you," Heather purred.

"It's not a gift," Wild Man said. "It marks you as part of us, as our property. No one outside of us can ever lay a hand on you, or say a hurtful word to you, but within our group, there is no limit to how you can be used. Are you ready for that?"

Heather shuddered, his feminine, waifish body tingling with a sensation that already neared ecstasy. "Yes, Sir," he purred.

"Are you ready to be initiated as our pet?"

Heather looked around. The private clubhouse was full of dangerous looking, leather-clad bikers, all wearing the flaming skulls of violators. Heather had thought of himself as their pet for a long time already. On his tummy, near his right hip, opposite the bondage fairy tattoo Tanya Payne had given him, was the tattoo of a naked redhead her hair a burning flame that engulfed both her and the motorcycle she straddled. "I'm ready," Heather purred.

"Get on your knees, slut," Wild Man commanded in a cold, formal voice.

Heather dropped to his pale knees on the dirty warehouse floor, looking up at the oldest of the bikers with trembling awe for the power and authority he could wield over rough and dangerous men, let alone wispy and waifish sissy dolls.

Wild Man reached down with a big, wide hand, knuckles swollen and fingers coarse, and he touched Heather's pretty face. The gentleness of the man's touch was shocking, and Heather nearly gasped as if he'd been doused in cold water.

Wild Man's big thumb traced the shemale's Botox filled lips, marking the edges of his beautiful, feminine features. Heather opened his mouth, his body surging with electric excitement, feeling the heat and pressure of the man's thumb barely brushing the pillows of his bright red lips. Wild Man released Heather's cheek and drew his hand back. He held his hand in the air for a moment, giving Heather a breath to prepare. Then Wild Man brought his hand down hard, slapping Heather hard across the face.

Heather shuddered with thrilling pleasure as the harsh, stinging blow rushed through his system. He purred as his cheek reddened. Wild man lowered his other hand and slapped Heather's beautiful face, just as roughly from the other side.

Heather's dick surged painfully in the chastity device, throbbing to get hard but helplessly locked up. Wild Man spoke in a loud, formal tone, looking out at the crowd. "I do what I want to weak little bitches."

Wild Man stepped aside, and another man stepped up, muscles and tattoos and black leather. The new man slapped Heather across the face as well. "I do what I want to weak little bitches," the biker announced. Another Violator stepped up from behind Heather. He grabbed the back of Heather's neck, making it hard to breathe as he pushed the sissy forward. Heather hovered as if about to spill forward onto his face, his weight held up by the biker's iron grip on his long, elegant neck. The biker slapped an open hand across the soft flesh of Heather's ass then growled, "I do what I want to weak little bitches." He jerked Heather upright once more then released him. Another hand hit Heather's ass, making it sting as another voice declared, "I do what I want to weak little bitches!"

Heather looked at Wild Man with wet, lustful eyes. Wild Man was watching with quiet authority. The man seemed completely unaffected accept for the bulge of a massive cock in his jeans. The biker beside Wild Man was opening his jeans and letting them fall to his ankles, his cock thick as beer can and bulging with veins. Heather stared at that beautiful, monstrous cock while more hands struck his pale, hormone softened flesh. Hands to the back of his head, to his ass and skinny thighs, to his cheeks and shoulders and back and tits. No one struck him with a closed fist, no one kicked or kneed or elbowed him, but the open hand blows were deliciously merciless, making his freckled skin turn red with stinging electricity. Heather pressed his palms to the dirty floor for balance as he leaned forward, arching his back while his body and face were smacked and slapped.

Voices echoed through the room as hands abused every inch of Heather's body. "I do what I want to weak little bitches." The bikers spoke at once, slapping him from multiple sides and different angles, voices overlapping, "I do what I want to weak little bitches."

Heather quivered in hunger and pain and the ecstasy of all that attention as his dick strained against its cage. He was crying, the thick eyeliner he wore over his subtle tattooed makeup was running, but he wasn't just crying from pain, he was crying from the joy of belonging. Someone grabbed Heather's soft hair and jerked his face back. The face of spike hovered over him. Spike growled, "I do what I want to weak little bitches," then spat in Heather's face.

Heather gasp as the spittle touched his supple skin. It hit just below his eye and dribbled towards his mouth. He licked it up as it touched his lush red lips. Hands continued to slap and pinch and squeeze his long, luscious curves as the first cock was pushed to his lips.

Heather parted his lips and extended his little pink tongue, pressing it to the underside of the cock as it moved into his wet mouth. The fat, beer-can cock stretched Heather's lips, drool running out the corners of his distorted mouth. "I do what I want to weak little bitches," the cocks owner grunted as he pressed it steadily deeper, pushing it into Heather's tight little throat.

Heather slurped greedily on the fat dick, his mouth flooding. The girth of the cock expanded Heather's throat as it moved through his esophagus. Rough hands split his tender ass-cheeks apart, exposing his smooth, bleached-pink asshole. Heather wiggled his curved ass enticingly, his body begging to be impaled on hot, throbbing cock. Dick plunged back and forth in Heather's throat, its owner grunting with animal pleasure. Heather could feel the presence of a man behind him as the heat of a swollen cock-head began pressing against the tender rosebud of his tight little sissy-pussy.

Heather's body quivered with anticipation, then shuddered with pain and satisfaction as the cock slammed forward. Heather's rectum exploded with sensation as it was pounded full of hard, hot meat. Heather rocked back against it, savoring pain and pleasure. The hard ridges of cock rubbed the tender contours of Heather's flesh, his tongue and his throat, his sphincter and his prostate. The two men began to pound both of Heather's tender holes, their hips slamming forward at differing rhythms. Hand's continued to slap, pinch and poke Heather's pale skin. Fingers twisted the pink nipples that capped his firm, fake tits. Heather's own penis ached, forced to say limp in its cage as it struggled to swell with excitement.

The men kept telling him, and the words echoed in his mind; "I do what I want to weak little bitches." Heather didn't really know anything about who he had been before Tanya Payne got her hands on him, but he was sure of one thing: He had always been a weak little bitch. Some deep part of him had always craved this, and at his core he deserved every filthy minute of it. He welcomed the warm throbbing of the cocks hammering his esophagus and colon. He craved the hands slapping him and the voices calling him names. He loved every minute of the humiliation and the pain.

Heather's long, lean, feminized body rocked back and forth as it was hammered in two opposing directions by rough, tattooed bikers. Slaps and pinches filled his awareness. His hair was tugged, and his tits were groped. Every inch of him was being fondled by big, powerful hands.

Almost at the same time, the two cocks began to erupt hot jets of semen deep into Heather's ass and throat. Every squirt was like a deep reward, penetrating his core, like Tanya's voice. Each powerful spray felt like Tanya whispering into his brain, "Good girl." Heather wasn't sure he would ever be completely free of that radiant goddess, or that he ever really wanted to. He rocked his body back and forth, his lips and asshole stretched around two cocks, eagerly milking out the last drops of their potent seed.

When the balls had been drained and the dicks softened slightly, they were pulled free of Heather's openings. Heather's ass leaked cum, which dribbled down his smooth, pink balls and ran in glistening strings to the floor. Heather waited, mouth open, ass gaping, sperm running out of his ass and cum dripping down his chin.

He didn't have to wait long for both his holes to be filled once more with fat, throbbing cock. Heather felt shudders of pleasure as the contours of strange dicks began to move inside him again. The men worked their hips and Heather worked his own slinky body, bouncing between them aggressively, driving their dicks deep down his throat and up his ass.

Heather felt blissful in the energy of that thick meat, sliding back and forth in his slick, filthy holes. He could feel the men's pleasure, radiating inside him, making his pleasure even more intense. He could feel the excitement of all those eyes, looking at his soft, perfectly feminized, cosmetically enhanced frame as it bounced between two cocks. He felt the warmth of hands, slapping and squeezing him, the warmth of attention, filling him with purpose.

Men waited in line to fuck him, as other men stroked themselves, fondling his pale, perfect flesh. Two more loads of thick, filthy cum exploded inside Heather's hungry sissy-cunt and thirsty throat. Heather gulped it down and soaked it up, grateful and warm and ready for more. Two more massive cocks plunged into both his ravaged holes and Heather attacked them with the same gleeful intensity, bouncing between them like a bimbo dance-queen or supercharged sex-robot.

The savage bikers hammered their thick cocks inside Heather, pummeling his openings with brutal thrusts, as

Heather worked his body back and forth, begging for more. Heather bounced between the two cocks with such lush, filthy energy, that they came within minutes, adding another layer of filth to Heather's hot little holes. As soon as those two men pulled out of Heather's body, two more took their place, savagely pounding their erections into the slinky sissy doll.

Heather loved the changing sensations of new cocks throbbing inside him. He gazed up at the biker who stuffed his throat, entreating the man with his eyes to slap him harder, to fuck him rougher, use him meaner, and call him dirtier names.

"Filthy sissy whore," the man grunted as he pounded Heather's esophagus. "Eat every inch of me, you nasty shemale trash."

Heather gobbled down the man's meat, drooling and slurping as his ass was drilled behind him, hands slapping and pinching and dicks being stroked all around him. Heather's prostate began to tingle with powerful vibrations. Jolts of electricity shot up his spine and shot in all directions through his brain, making his whole-body spasm. Heather's limp dick twitched in his cock-cage as his balls tightened. All Heather's muscles trembled and flexed as he began to spray thick wads of cum threw the hole in the end of his chastity device. He sprayed hot sperm against his own tummy and in arcs onto the floor. The dick in his mouth was jerked free and strings of hot jizz began to splatter across his lovely face and into his open mouth. The taste of that salty sperm made Heather's body shudder even deeper as his orgasm intensified.

Heather's ass began to flood with more semen as the man ejaculated with a grunt. Heather had taken so many loads inside his sissy-womb that he was overflowing, and the force of that new load seemed to hammer inside him with deep hydraulic pressure. Heather whimpered in his surgically modified, highly trained voice; a voice that was more simpering, high and feminine than most natural women could achieve. Men began to orgasm all around him, shooting off their wads in thick bursts that felt hot and thrilling against Heather's pale, abused flesh.

Hot sprays of dozens of men began to fire off one by one, two by two, and three by three. All around him hot jets of spunk showered down. Heather wiggled his long, lithe body beneath the rain of sperm, arching his back as it splattered against his slim frame. He parted his lips and turned his face up, letting it land in his mouth and decorate his gorgeous face.

His skin glistened with thick, creamy jizz as it coated his frame and dribbled from his body to the floor. He felt like he'd been wrestling in warm milk mixed with hot oil, his body shining with a filthy glaze. Heather sat back on his heels, wearing nothing but his "Sissy-Pet" choker and the contents of over twenty men's balls. He rubbed the milky sperm into his flesh, bringing his hands to his gorgeous perky tits, and massaging them till they too were glazed in cum. Heather's red hair was a shade darker, now that it was dripping wet with semen.

Wild Man stepped forward once more as the men all backed away. He held his massive cock in his hand, still hard. Heather realized his was the one cock he had yet to service tonight. Heather gave the man a charming smile, hand squeezing his own tits and skin covered in an oily sheen.

Wild Man stepped up to Heather and Heather pressed his palms to the man's hairy thigh, gazing up at him with submissive hunger. Wild Man gave the little sissy a tiny head-nod. Heather wrapped a hand around the man's shaft and wrapped lips around his tip. Heather's lips and tongue were slick with semen, making the cock glide with ease into his mouth and down his throat. Heather squeezed his shaft, hand following behind his cum-glazed, Botox-filled lips as they cradled the bulging contours. Heather's head bobbed with eager, intensity, still as hungry for the last drop of semen as he had been for the first. He gazed up at the powerful older man, begging to be fed one more time.

Wild Man smiled back. He didn't touch Heather's filthy face or hair, but he watched with affection as the tranny gobbled up his meat. Heather's head bounced on the man's dick, slurping it in and out of his throat with loud, wet noises. Heather let his lips smack as they slipped off Wild Man's pole and he began to swirl his pink tongue around the bulging purple tips, slathering it in saliva and semen. He sucked the cock back into his mouth once more and rocked his body forward, plunging the hot meat down his sperm-coated throat again.

Wild Man inhaled deeply. "Good girl," he said. "That's a good girl."

Heather looked up at him, stroking his shaft and sucking just the tip.

"Yes," Wild Man said. "That's a good girl."

The sound of the man's deep, powerful voice was so calm and commanding that it made Heather shudder once more, his body tingling as if he was going to orgasm all over again. That is exactly what happened. As the man began to explode hot cum into Heather's mouth, Heather's balls and anus vibrated with intensity and warmth, his body tingled with ecstasy and his mind went blank.

Heather's well-trained body worked on auto-pilot, gulping down Wild Man's cum and jerking his shaft, but his brain was a thousand miles away, sailing over the highway, riding on the back of a flaming motorcycle.

When Heather's mind returned to reality, he looked up at the leader of the biker's and he smiled with grateful awe at the man. Wild Man smiled down at the cum-splattered redhead once more and said, "Welcome to the family, little sissy pet."

Filthily Ever After

Jen listened to Tanya Payne's sensuous voice. On the table across from him was the gorgeous Asian doll he loved. Ting stared blankly ahead, wires attached to her head, monitoring and altering the electrical currents of her brain. Tubes ran into Ting's arms, filling her with intense mind altering and pleasure enhancing drugs. She was naked except for a sheath that covered her erection, stimulating and shocking it as necessary, and a plug going up her tender pink asshole, capable of delivering the same sensations whenever Tanya Payne deemed it appropriate.

Jen knew he was in the same condition and would have the same dazed mindless look in his eyes soon.

"Yes," Ting moaned in her delicious, accented voice. "I will serve you forever Mistress. I will never stray again."

"Good girl," Tanya Payne purred, her tall, luscious body hovering over both sissies. She wore an elegant but tightly fitting blouse and skirt that made her look like a powerful executive from a high budget porn. She nodded at Bridget, who wore her slinky little nurse's uniform. Bridget turned up the pleasure dials on the machine and Ting writhed in orgasm.

Tanya Payne watched the lush Asian doll twist and shudder in her restraints. Tanya had a small, twisted smile and a distant look on her beautiful, cold face. She touched Ting's breasts, feeling the hard, pink nipples and making Ting tremble even harder. "Good, good girl," Tanya purred.

When Ting's trembling climax ended, and she became limp and blank once more, Tanya had her table wheeled away by a muscle-bound guard and turned her attention to Jen.

"My sweet, sweet little doll," Tanya Payne purred. "Whatever possessed you to try and leave me?"

"I don't remember," Jen answered honestly.

Tanya adjusted a loose strand of Jen's long, blonde hair. "That's good," she said. "That's very good. You don't need to remember that. You only need to remember the sound of my voice and the feeling of my power."

"Thank you," Jen said, relieved not to have to remember.

"But I am going to have to hurt you. I do it out of love. But I have to hurt you just the same."

Jen trembled with fear and excitement. For some reason, when Tanya talked of suffering, she made it sound delicious.

"Are you ready, Sweetie?" Tanya asked. "Are you ready for me to hurt you now?"

Jen's dick was hard in its sheath and his skin tingled with goose-bumps. "Yes," he said.

"I'm going to hurt you," Tanya said. "But first I want you to picture a blinking light..."

Jen began to picture everything Tanya Payne instructed him to. He imagined blinking lights counting up, and stairs counting down, and mile posts drifting by. He listened to Tanya's lush hypnotic voice and drifted into a deep, distant trance.

"Now," Tanya spoke directly into his brainwashed, bimbo mind, "I want you to picture yourself on the highway somewhere all alone. I am far away. Even my voice feels distant as if speaking to you through a long, dark tunnel."

"I see it," Jen moaned.

Tanya nodded at Bridget and Bridget smiled with wicked excitement. The petite brunette's nipples were hard as ice, pressing against the thin fabric of her skin-tight nurse's uniform as she began turning the shock dials on her control panel.

As Jen writhed on the table, feeling the painful electricity shoot through him, he remembered how much he hated to be alone, away from the strict, thrilling control of his goddess, Tanya Payne.

Bridget watched Jen's body twist and shake. The dark-haired tranny's big dick was getting hard, pressing against her uniform, making a clear, distinct bulge. Every ridge and vein was visible through the taught fabric of Bridget's uniform as her hardon pulsed between it and her tummy. Her beautiful eyes shined with lust as she watched Jen whimper and shake on the table.

Tanya watched Jen suffer with the dispassionate look of a scientist. After a long moment she nodded at the slim shemale nurse. Bridget reluctantly turned down the pain dials, bringing Jen back to a relaxed state of calm. Tanya eyed her slinky assistant for a minute, her stare lingering over the bulge in the tranny's dress before returning to study Jen once more.

Jen was breathing deeply, an intense feeling of relief washing over him as the electricity died.

"Now," Tanya purred into his feeble, brainwashed mind. "I want you to picture yourself in room full of beautiful manakins. You are walking through them, their smooth plastic curves pressing against your skin as you push through the crowd of them. My voice is no longer far away, but it is everywhere, it is coming from all directions and even from inside you."

Jen pictured a vast space, the smooth curves of manakin bodies pressing against his lush, curved frame as he moved through the crowd.

Tanya purred, "As you move through the manakins they become more real, more lifelike, softer and lusher. They purr as you touch them, and they touch you back; a crowd of beautiful synthetic dolls, touching you and touching each other."

Jen's dick throbbed as he imagined himself moving through the crowd, pressing through the wall of beautiful synthetic flesh.

"You look around and you see your face on all of them. Everyone is touching and kissing, and my voice is moving through everyone's blank little mind, telling you all what to do."

The sheath on Jen's cock was vibrating and pulsating with warmth, as the plug in his ass began to tingle against his sphincter. He could feel all those hands and bodies, pressing against him. Lips and fingers and little pink dicks, pushing against his flesh as he moved through the crowd.

"You are moving across all that soft, supple flesh; brushing past tits and lush, curving asses. Little erections are poking you, fingers caressing you, lips brushing your flesh. You move through the crowd and it gets thicker and thicker until you reach the center of the room. Here is where my voice is the loudest."

Jen imagined himself standing in the center of that room, touching and being touched by hundreds of hormone-softened, surgically enhanced bodies, the thrilling sound of Tanya Payne's voice washing over him. The sheath on his dick was vibrating faster, the plug in his ass sending throbbing jolts of tingling electricity pulsating through his rectum.

Tanya watched Jen's body trembling in ecstasy beneath her. Her hands idly traced the sissy's curves, caressing supple flesh. Tanya bit her lower lip, breathing increasing, her pussy flooding with excitement and filling the room with its scent. "Doesn't it feel good?" Tanya purred. "Doesn't it feel good to be part of that soft wall of flesh? Doesn't it feel good to belong to me?"

"Yes," Jen moaned. "It feels like paradise."

"Good girl," Tanya purred. She nodded at Bridget who turned up all the pleasure levels on the control panel. Jen whimpered as sensation overtook him, overloading his needy little body with tingling pleasure. Tanya continued to watch her model-perfect, feminized sex-doll. She brought one hand up under her skirt, feeling her own dripping panties. Tanya pushed her panties aside and felt the silky flesh of her pink pussy. She exhaled deeply as she pressed her fingers inside her warm, wet cunt. "Good girl," she moaned again.

Jen imagined himself moving in the warm, titillating light of the Goddess's voice, telling him he was a good girl. He imagined himself with an erection in each hand, his body squeezed between the luscious curves of a hundred copies of himself.

Tanya looked at Bridget. She looked at the shemale nurses trim little frame and small, perky tits. She looked at the tranny's hard cock throbbing against the fabric of her skin-tight uniform. "Come here, Sweetie," she commanded.

Jen continued to writhe and whimper on the table he was strapped to, lost in the vivid hypnotic, drug-induced fantasies he was experiencing as the toys worked his penis and ass.

Bridget stepped up to her mistress, gazing up at the tall, radiant blonde. Tanya caressed the little tranny's pretty face, then pulled her closer. They pressed their lips together and began to kiss. Tanya's fingertips came to the hem of Bridget's nurses dress and pulled it up.

As Bridget's dress was raised above her tiny waist, her big erection popped free. Her beautiful dick was perfectly balanced and throbbing with power. She wore tiny pink panties that only covered her smooth, hairless balls. The beautiful shemale's dark skin was flawless and soft as Tanya kept pulling the dress up.

Tanya pulled the dress all the way off her little doll and threw it aside. Bridget's small chest was tall and firm, nipples dark and hard, her body slinky and petite, ribs expanding and contracting as she breathed deep with excitement. Tanya smiled and began to open her own blouse with torturous deliberation, slowly beginning to reveal the tantalizing view of her fantastic tits.

Bridget bit her lip, squeaking with need as she watched her mistress slowly strip.

Jen continued to wiggle and whimper on the table, imagining a pulsing, throbbing room of flesh, rubbing against him as his dick and asshole pulsated with heat and vibration.

Tanya's lush, curved body shimmered with perfection, her perfect pussy glistening as she stripped out of the last shred of her clothes. Bridget stared at the goddess drooling, her own tight little frame wiggling with excitement. Tanya stepped forward and pushed Bridget down onto the clean-white tile floor. Tanya straddled the petite shemale, lowering her lush frame down on Bridget's throbbing prick.

Bridget whimpered as her big erection began to pierce Tanya's hot, wet opening. Tanya lowered herself slowly down, savoring every inch of her doll's rock-hard cock. Tanya gripped Bridget's petite breasts, squeezing them in her soft hands. Tanya purred as she rolled her hips, driving Bridget's hot meat inside her. Her long body rolled and flexed as she rode the little tranny, blonde hair streaming down her slender back.

"My beautiful dolls," Tanya moaned. "My beautiful little toys. Good girls."

Bridget moaned, wiggling her body against her mistress, as Jen writhed on the table beside them. Bridget's gorgeous cock moved through the soft pink flesh of Tanya's delicious cunt, its contours slippery from glistening pussy-juice. Tanya rocked up and down, her seemingly endless legs spread out across the floor. Bridget gazed lovingly at her mistress, whimpering with each movement of the woman's curving hips.

"Thank you, Mistress," Bridget moaned. "Thank you, Goddess."

Tanya's flawless, natural breasts rolled and jiggled as her body rocked and writhed with increasing speed.

Jen whimpered and moaned. "Thank you, Goddess," he purred as he imagined his body being caressed by endless flesh. Doll hands squeezed his erection, stroking him with tender care as his own fingers gripped slim, sissy hardons. "Thank you, Goddess." He could hear his goddess moaning with pleasure, her breathing increasing. The pulse of all those synthetic sex-dolls increased, wiggling together faster as their mistress grew more aroused.

"Yes," Tanya moaned, her blonde hair whipping her chest and shoulders as she began to bounce on the petite shemale beneath her. "Good girl. Good dolly."

Bridget's cock pulsated and throbbed in Tanya's wet cunt. Three sensual, feminine voices whimpered in unison, but only one was actually female. Tanya ran her hands across her own lush curves and through her lustrous hair, her eyes closing as she shuddered with more and more pleasure.

Jen imagined himself grinding against all those perfect copies of his feminized self as the vibrations gyrating though his ass and across his dick merged and increased in intensity. He listened to Tanya Payne's voice, which traveled along those vibrations, and touched every flawless creature in the room. "Yes," he whimpered. "Thank you, Goddess." He took a deep breath, his luscious artificial breasts raising as he began to orgasm.

Tanya's powerful, sensual voice moaned in ecstasy as Bridget shuddered beneath her.

"Yes," Bridget cried. "Yes."

Tanya bounced on the shemale harder, slamming her body down on the tranny's slinky little frame. "Mmmm," Tanya purred as Bridget began to whimper and cum, filling her magnificent pussy with hot jets of cream. Tanya rode the small t-girl as she bucked beneath her, Bridget shivering as she emptied her balls.

Tanya's head turned up and her back arched, her gorgeous tits pushed out in front of her as she too began to climax. Bridget shuddered out the last spurts of her semen, then relaxed with a sigh, crying tears of joy. Tanya flipped forward, whipping her blonde hair across Bridget's face as she grabbed the small tranny by the chin and kissed her possessively.

"Good girl," Tanya purred again before she stood up.

Tanya moved to Jen's table and slipped on top of the feminized doll, straddling his face. She lowered her pussy down to Jen's lips. Jen didn't need to be told what to do. Without hesitation he opened his mouth, tasted Tanya's magnificent cunt, and began to slurp up the mess that Bridget had made.

Time passed.

Jen had no idea how much time had passed; Months, years, decades, days. It didn't matter. The only thing that mattered was pleasure. The pleasure Jen gave his Mistress by serving her clients, and the pleasure Jen received by being useful to important men.

He was standing outside of one of Tanya's playrooms. Tanya was reminding him who he was.

"You are a brand-new bride on your wedding night," Tanya purred into Jen's vacant mind. "You can't wait to please your new husband and his other bride. The three of you had a beautiful ceremony and are excited about starting your romantic and passionate three-way marriage."

Jen realized now why she felt so excited. It was her wedding night. She ran her hands down her fit, luscious frame, feeling the lace and silk of her wedding dress. The dress was virgin white, but incredibly short and tight. She loved the way it hugged her flesh, pushing against her tits and against her panties, pressing against her tingling clit. She turned to her left and realized she was not alone. Her new wife was beside her.

The gorgeous, lushly built Asian also wore a slutty little wedding dress. The two brides held hands and gazed into each other's eyes. "I'm so happy," Jen told Ting.

"Me too," Ting purred. "Let's go see our husband."

They walked hand in hand into the playroom.

Their handsome husband was already naked, waiting in the heart-shaped bed. He was older, perhaps in his fifties, but he was large and powerful, fit and clean. He seemed to radiate power and success. He had a full head of greyish hair. The salt and pepper hairs that covered his chest also ran down in a thin line from his abs to his buzz cut pubic hair. His big, masculine cock was still limp, resting against his muscular thigh like a calm but dangerous snake. He watched them as they strolled into the room hand in hand.

Jen smiled demurely at the man. The man looked at them.

"Amazing," he said. "Absolutely perfect."

Ting and Jen both blushed.

"My lovely brides," he said. "Why don't you help each other get undressed?"

Ting and Jen both bowed slightly to the man, then they turned to each other. Jen's fingers were trembling as she reached forward and touched the lace of Ting's luxurious, tight dress. She traced the fabric up Ting's incredibly slender sides to the dramatic curve of her fantastic rack. She gazed into the lovely Asian bride's cleavage, mouthwatering. Ting leaned in, taking a firm hold of Jen's rounded ass, squeezing the soft flesh as she pulled Jen tight against her and kissed her lips.

Jen felt herself melt against her wife's kiss, their luscious tits pressing together as their tongues flickered into each other's mouths. Ting's hands caressed up the curve of Jen's ass, across the small of her back, then rose up her spine to the zipper of her dress. Jen felt her clit get rock hard in her panties, throbbing with need as the two bride's bodies wiggled against each other. Ting clasped the silver zipper and began to pull it down. The tight dress spread apart as the zipper opened, revealing Jen's supple, slinky back. Jen wiggled out of the dress and let it fall to the floor. She stood there in just her heels, white silk nylon stockings, garters and white lace panties. The very tip of Jen's pink clit was poking out the top of her panties, throbbing with need as she grabbed Ting's hips and pulled her close once more.

The two wives kissed again, their Botox-filled lips mashing together as their tongues collided in each other's wet mouths. Jen put one hand on Ting's lush ass as her other hand began to pull at the zipper of her dress. Soon Ting too was naked except for matching panties, stockings and heels.

Jen grabbed the girls big, artificial breasts once more. She mashed them together and bent forward, pressing her beautiful face between the lush mounds. The softness of the brown breasts against Jen's soft face was thrilling. Jen could feel her blonde locks tickling the Asian's flesh as she moved her lips to one of Ting's nipples and began to suckle. Jen moved from nipple to nipple, flicking the hard buttons with her tongue and nibbling at the pink flesh.

Ting moaned then grabbed Jen's face with both hands and jerked her face up, kissing her.

On the heart-shaped newlywed bed, their groom was hard as a rock, watching his two wives kiss. The two brides kissed and caressed each other, tits mashed together, erections barely poking out the tops of their bridal panties.

Jen kissed Ting's slender brown neck, then lowered her mouth, kissing the Asian's hormone softened mocha skin. The slender blonde found her way to Ting's breasts once more, kissing them each and giving each pink nipple a flick with her little wet tongue. Jen kissed down Ting's impossibly tiny torso, lips caressing her sunken tummy till she reached the tip of her clit, barely poking out from her panties.

Jen pressed her lush, Botox-filled lips to the tip Ting's little pink erection, leaving it glistening with spittle. Jen looked up at her wife, fingers teasing up the Asian's slender legs. Jen unclipped Ting's garters then began to peel her panties down. The Asian's rock-hard clit popped free, bouncing against Jen's silky blonde hair. Jen peeled the panties down past Ting's heels. Jen unhooked the buckles and straps on Ting's sexy shoes. Ting lifted each foot and Jen slid off each shoe. Jen smiled up at her Asian bride as she began to roll her nylon stockings down, exposing the bare flesh of her smooth, brown legs.

Ting stepped out of her panties and nylons, standing naked, her clit hard and throbbing. Jen moved her mouth to Ting's erection and sucked it in, drool running down to the beautiful girl's tiny balls. Jen swallowed Ting's clit, then swallowed her balls as well, her tongue flicking the Asian's smooth taint.

Ting whimpered in a weak, feminine voice as the gorgeous blonde swallowed her complete sex. With Ting's little meat and balls in Jen's mouth, there was nothing to make the Asian look the slightest bit unnatural, her hands in Jen's hair, her big, artificial tits rising as she moaned. She looked like any other young, Asian bride, another woman's mouth on her hot, little crotch.

Jen swished spit across Ting's clit, sucking the Asian's erection and balls at the same time, swirling her tongue around the Asian's tiny balls and teasing the girl's taint.

Ting couldn't seem to take the teasing sensation of her clit being swirled in Jen's spit-filled mouth. She pushed Jen to her back on the floor and straddled her. The two wives kissed again, then Ting sat up and pulled Jen's panties down below the blonde's clit and balls. Ting scooted up, the two wives tiny balls mashing together, their clits touching. Ting reached down and squeezed both of their erections together. The lustrous Asian doll squeezed both hard clits in her hand, pressing them tight in her fist as she began to stroke up and down.

Ting's clit was still dripping wet from Jen's mouth, and all that saliva served to make both pole's slippery as Ting squeezed and stroked them, mashing them together as if they were one, little dick. Ting arched her back and turned her face down, spitting a long line of glistening saliva down onto her hand and both throbbing clits. She looked back up at Jen with a wicked smile.

Both girls gazed into each other's eyes, making faces of pleasure as Ting's hand moved across the pink flesh of both tiny erections. Ting squeezed hard, tits jiggling as her hand jerked, smiling at her brand-new wife.

Jen looked up in that beautiful face. How long had she known her new bride? It seemed like they had been connected forever. Perhaps even longer than their husband, who Jen loved deeply, but who's face and features kept shifting and changing. She looked over at the man now, his massive cock in his hand as he watched his new wives play on the floor of the newlywed suite. "Come play with us, Daddy," Jen whimpered.

The man stepped off the bed, his big body and huge cock radiating power. Ting began to peel Jen's panties down with one hand, her other hand still gripping both their clits, mashing them together. The big man stood over them both, Ting slipped her knees between Jen's long legs and leaned forward, exposing her little pink asshole as she kissed Jen once more, hand working both erections between their slim, feminine bodies.

The man looked down at Ting, naked and brown with tiny features and dramatic curves, writhing completely naked over Jen, who still wore her heels and stockings and had her bridal panties stretched across her thighs. He watched as his two new brides wiggled against each other, tits and balls rubbing. Jen slithered out of her panties and wrapped her long legs around Ting, crossing her ankles behind the Asians slinky back.

The man knelt behind them and began to rub his fat cock along Ting's smooth crack.

Jen could feel Ting's balls flutter against her own. She could feel the little Asian's breathing change as she felt their new husband's big, throbbing meat pressing against her tight, warm opening. The man leaned forward, pressing his weight down on Ting's brown back. Jen uncrossed her ankles, then wrapped her legs around both bodies, pulling them both towards her slinky frame. The man reached between the two luscious bodies beneath him, grabbing one of Ting's lush artificial tits with one hand, and one of Jen's with the other.

As the man began to penetrate Ting, she buried her face in the crook of Jen's long neck, whimpering with painful excitement. Jen lifted her face and kissed her new husband over Ting's shoulder, his weight pressing the soft Asian down on her. Ting's hand was still wedged between their smooth bodies, squeezing both their erections as her body began to rock, their husband moving inside her.

"Yes," Ting whimpered. "Oh, shit yes."

The man's deep voice groaned, his tongue plunging into Jen's mouth as his strong lips mashed down against her lush, Botox-enhanced pillows.

"It hurts so good," Ting purred. "His big, manly cock feels so amazing in my tight little cunt."

Jen could imagine the satisfying sensation of fat dick so vividly, that she knew she was no virgin. Jen couldn't remember anything but this night, and she didn't need to. This was her magic night. Her special night. The romantic three-way marriage she had been dreaming of since she was a little girl.

"Yes," Ting whimpered, her body rocking back and forth against Jen as the man's dick slid through her soft, pink rectum.

Jen could feel Ting pushing her ass back, trying to force their husband deeper, trying to make her cunt more accessible. Jen unlocked her long legs from around both bodies. She let Ting pull back, pushing onto her hands and knees so the cock could impale her that much harder. The man rose with her, working his hips harder, grunting as he took hold of the Asian's tiny waist and began to pound her.

Jen slithered on her back, spinning around beneath the bodies so that she could bring her face close to the action. She slid till she was directly under Ting's ass, watching it being violated by their new husband's fat, throbbing cock.

Jen took her own clit in one hand and Ting's clit in the other. She squeezed both erections with two fingers, jerking herself and Ting simultaneously as she watched her wife get impaled by her husband. Ting's lush ass-cheeks smashed down against their husbands' strong body, her tiny pink balls being slapped with his massive, hairy sack as he drove his impressive meat deep into her tender asshole.

Ting whimpered. She lowered her face, and kissed Jen's balls with fluttering affectionate lips. She lapped at Jen's balls between wet whimpers as her asshole was violated. She kissed

Jen's taint, her plump lips and wet tongue teasing Jen's delicate flesh.

Jen purred. She could feel the Asian's dark hair, silky against her smooth thighs as the skilled little mouth licked, sucked and kissed her. Jen began kissing Ting's balls to return the favor, still jerking both their slender poles.

The man hammered Ting's asshole harder, grunting like an animal as he grew faster and more forceful. Ting cried out in a deliciously submissive, feminine whimper with each thrust. Then, each time the dick began to slide back out of the gorgeous Asian's ass, she eagerly kissed Jen's asshole. Ting's lips cradled Jen's rosebud, and Ting drove her tongue inside, eating Jen's ass with spirited enthusiasm between each, pain-filled, ecstasy driven whimper.

"Yes," the man grunted, pounding Ting's ass.

Jen worked both hands, jerking her and Ting with the same increasing rhythm. She licked Ting's balls and taint and slurped her wet tongue across their husband's shaft as it hammered back and forth. She kissed and licked their husband's fat, hairy sack.

Ting cried out, "Shit!" then made a loud slurping noise as she drove her tongue in Jen's asshole. "Fuck!" then lapped wetly across the flesh of Jen's sphincter.

Jen squeezed her fingers, feeling the pulse of both throbbing clits in her hands, savoring the resistance of the cartilage. She could feel the vibration of their husband's cock ramming in Ting's rectum as the force vibrated through the sexy Asian's hard little clit.

Ting raised her face now, arching her back, she held her body up by gripping Jen's slender, model-perfect legs. She began to bounce back against her man, her tits and balls jiggling as she worked herself against his big, fat cock. Jen continued to stroke both clits, watching her wife get hammered above her, curling up so she could kiss both pairs of balls.

Jen could feel herself getting close to cumming, but more importantly she could feel her husband and wife getting close to cumming. She relaxed her body, stroking both clits and laying her head down on the floor so she could focus on just watching her man pound her wife's luscious ass.

It was a beautiful show, Ting's lush body rocking back and forth above her, pressing against their man as he fucked her like a beast, his big hands locked around her shrunken waist.

Suddenly the man Jerked his cock back. He pulled it all the way out of Ting's asshole and he gripped it in his own fist. He began to jerk himself.

Jen stared up at that massive dick, hovering over her face, its tip pointing right between her beautiful blue eyes. The man continued jerking, pointing his staff at Jen's face. He gripped his meat hard, groaning as the first spray of hot, salty cum sprayed down on Jen's pretty face. Jen gasped, that first wad of semen was huge and overwhelming, hitting Jen like a hot pie in the face. Jen instantly began to cum. She fired hot cream against Ting's tits and against her own body, drenching her tummy and even her own tits with forceful sprays of jizz. Ting cried out and began to orgasm too, writhing above Jen, she started shooting her hot spunk down on Jen's chest.

Jen was being showered in semen.

Her own clit was shooting spurts of cum across her flesh, splattering her tummy, ribcage and the underside of her tits. Ting's throbbing clit was hitting Jen's luscious tits from above, drenching her nipples and coating her mounds like snow-capped mountains. The man was jizzing all over Jen's face and into her eager, open mouth. Jen gulped down mouthful after mouthful of sticky cream, but still the man continued to unload his balls.

Jen wasn't sure how many times she'd been cum on in her life, but she was sure she'd never been cummed on like this before. She felt like the living, breathing center of one continuous climax; shaking in ecstasy as strings of pure, delicious pleasure splattered against her slender, feminine body. She writhed as wave after wave of thick, hot sperm shot down across her supple, hormone-enriched skin. She continued to jerk herself with one hand as she released Ting's clit with her other hand and began to rub her own cum-glazed tits. Strings of filthy jizz continued raining down on her. She swallowed it, savoring the salty musk, then opened her mouth again to catch more. She rubbed it into her tits and into the skin of her long, graceful neck. She writhed in ecstasy as she shot out, showered in, and swallowed down the last evidence of three intense orgasms.

As the shower stopped, Ting spun around so they were face to face and pressed her lush body down. The sperm made Jen's body slippery, and Ting's flesh slid easily across Jen's slickness as if they were wrestling in oil. Jen was still writhing in blissful aftershocks as Ting's tits smashed down on hers, greasy pink nipples rubbing together. Their little spent dicks pressed together; limp and slippery, covered in cream. Ting's luscious red lips pressed against Jen's cum-splattered lips. Ting pushed her tongue into Jen's mouth and they kissed passionately.

After the kiss, Ting purred. "I love you."

"I love you too," Jen moaned.

Their husband laughed. “I love both of you filthy little fuck-things.”

They both looked up at him, smiling with endless and unrestrained affection at the older man. “We love you too, Daddy,” the two filthy little fuck-things purred in unison, their lips shinning with cum and lip-gloss.

The End

Visit

JennaMastersErotica.blogspot.com

For links to all my other stories, series and collections

Printed in Great Britain
by Amazon

39203755R00088